Potpourri

Also by Rick Lawton

The Rex
Chasing Lazarus
Rex Stories
Phisto

Potpourri

Rick Lawton

Sasha Press
San Francisco, CA
www.sashapress.com

Published 2021

Published by Sasha Press
San Francisco
www.sashapress.com

ISBN-13: 978-0-9788862-5-7
Printed in the United States of America

Contents

Potpourri

Live out of your imagination, not your history

Steven Covey

Prelude

Let's get down to it! Funny, that is completely atypical. I always procrastinate. I'm wishy-washy. I hem and haw. I go this way, stop before my supposed goal, then turn around and go in the opposite direction. Several of the women I've known have commented on my delaying tactics, ad infinitum.

See, I did it again!

Getting-down-to-it. I'm older now. I hesitate to say how old. Let's call it seniorish. Who would have expected it? Many seniorish people feel a rumble in their guts and a missing part of their puzzle. In other words, they feel a pressing need to track down how they got where they are. They plant themselves in the local historical society and dig deep into withered roots, noting the movements, marriages, deaths, wrongs, and rights of their ancestors. What are they trying to find? What difference would it make in their lives? Perhaps it makes for fodder when they lean back in their chairs, adjust the cushions, and philosophize about the billionaire manqué four or five generations ago or, heh-heh, the bank robber or clichéd horse thief.

What about me? I look back in the same way I look into the future. I look back using an overactive imagination and fashion scenes and people and words and names in the same way I fashion future events. There is an inconclusiveness about life—even when we're in the thick of things and stuff happens that is indelibly printed on our souls. We try to think of how things were in that clear-eyed stand-out moment, and our memories are fuzzy, and they get fuzzier every second until that past dramatic event is just another present-day fantasy.

You can see this is leading into stories. Stories imagine how we were/are/will be—that's the premise. So, the stories in this collection imagine how I was, or how I thought, or how I fantasized at a particular place and time. You know, the stories continually surprise me. Did I really think like that, worry like that, imagine like that?

Let's start with names. Let's start with the name Mathew Hopkins. Mathew...or is that Matt...or is that Cat? Let's find out who I was or who I may have been in the first story, "Name Game."

Name Game

Where were our orders?

Some monkey, somewhere, was matching needs—short order cooks, drivers, clerks...—with draftees. At Fort Dix, we were trained for one thing: infantry. Our life expectancy in a fire fight in Nam ranged from five seconds to twenty depending on who you asked. We were scared shitless. We walked around like zombies, smoking cigarettes, drinking black coffee, getting drunk in the beer halls. Then some of us shipped out. After two weeks, there was a core—we were in the college-op officers program but decided not to opt—of ten of us stuck in limbo.

Where were our orders?

A week later, I jumped out of a deuce-and-a-half and lined up before a flag, which flapped slowly in front of the main building of the 13th USA Artillery Detachment right outside Kever, Germany. An hour later, I sat on a hard bed and stared at summer light streaming through the quaint window with the odd hinges. For the first time in five months, I took a breath. I wasn't going to Nam, and I wasn't going to die.

That first night, I played pool in the rec room. Someone who was about to leave—I think it was Mike Barrett—called me "Cat." I think he called me that because of the way I walked around the pool table figuring my shots. The name stuck for two years.

***

No one, not even the officers if they'd been honest, took the 13th USA Arty Det seriously. The detachment was a Cold War backwash where we draftees—the college kids, the streetwise Italians from New York and New Jersey, the Hispanics from L.A., the hillbillies from Appalachia—watched the late sixties, the war, the protests, and the body bags as if it were a film unfolding frame by frame in a world from which we had been banished.

Boredom replaced apprehension and fear. "Cat" Hopkins replaced the bushy-tailed radical Mathew Hopkins, who had graduated from the University of Iowa. Mathew—Matt to my friends, Matty to Amy—had morphed into Cat, an American soldier, an ambiguous entity.

On leaves and furloughs, I took trips through Germany, Denmark, and France. But those breaks were few, and for most of the next two years, I played the role of Cat at the 13th USA Arty Det. And Army time, the base time, was infinite, a long road stretching beyond the horizon. I spent days juggling secret codes as a newly minted cryptographer, nights drinking or playing games. When I think about it, games became a symbol not just of Army life with its quaint customs of order and command but of life writ large.

It was fitting that my big change started with a game, a Ping-Pong game, and a rematch with Kurt, a German truck driver and Flugplatz Ping-Pong champ.

It was after Christmas, cold and wet. That day, I spent desultory hours in the crypto room breaking messages and an equally desultory time hanging out with Pellet, the HQ clerk. At five I closed and locked the crypto room and

14

changed into my jeans and T-shirt, had a pre-game shot of Jack Daniels, stuffed my paddle in my jeans, and walked to the rec room. The rec room was a huge room in the front of the main building with two pool tables at the far end, a bunch of sofas, a boombox, and three Ping-Pong tables at the near end. Two rows of eyeshade lamps descended like skinny glowing stalactites and ran from one end of the rec room to the other.

That night the rec room was thronged with semi-tanked GIs and Germans in green and gray fatigues, shouting and yelling in knots of two or three. Twenty surrounded the best Ping-Pong table, which was near the right wall. One of those eyeshade lamps lighted the table, and in the match the ball would disappear in the bulb and explode back, as if it had been sucked into a passing white hole and spit back out.

Kurt had a ruddy, dirty face and long brown hair, which flopped into his eyes. He took out his paddle and I took out mine, just like a scene from High Noon.

We fought through four games and won two apiece. The score dipped back and forth that fifth game, until we were down to the last point. The yelling stopped. It was my ad. My serve was weak and Kurt came back with his bad-ass overspin, and I barely caught the ball six feet behind the table. I lobbed it back full of devilish backspin. I knew it was short, but it got trapped in that light. It seemed to hang forever in some alternate universe, but finally it dropped like a stone and hit the net. With that backspin, I knew it was coming down on my side. We both watched it shimmy along the top. Finally it curled down on Kurt's side, as if it were tired, and dribbled off the table.

My point, my game. I pumped my fist in the air. The

Germans shook their heads. The boozed-up GIs let out a roar.

"Cat, Cat, Cat!"

"He's our man, if he can't do it..."

"The canteen! The canteen!"

To win or not to win. Deep questions didn't have a toe-hold in Kever, especially in the canteen. The canteen was at the other end of that same building. When we stormed in, it was in its usual merry state with holdover Christmas lights strung through the bar, Spec 4s banging on the pre-deluge Bally pinball, and the bubble-box juke belting out tail-end Aquarius 45s. The bar itself was a shallow L, and I liked to station myself near the elbow where I could watch the rest of the bar and the people passing the door.

My victory felt good—great. You can always slough it off and say it didn't mean a rat's ass, but winning at anything always makes you feel good. Johnny Mets, a Spec 5, bought me a beer and pounded on my back for a few minutes. It was us against them and we won. We always do.

After an hour, I had three empty bottles of Kever stacked on the bar. I was slightly tipsy and happy. Why not? What else was there to do when you were in the middle of nowhere?

"Frog" Packard, a bowlegged Louisianan, appeared in the doorway. Over his shoulder, through a corridor window, the fog made hazy vortices of the lights along the road that bound the detachment to the main base and the outside world. Beyond the lights were dairy farms, and ten flat miles beyond the farms was the North Sea. Even in winter, fog snuck off the North Sea and crept over farmlands and towns. Sometimes you couldn't see for ten feet. Once, the deuce-and-a-half, which ferried sad-faced GIs ten miles to the Nike-Hercules range, ran right off the road and hit a cow. I heard about it, but Pellet, the company clerk, had to write it up.

Frog took off his cap and angled around a squad of guards snapping their fingers to "Breakdown." He clapped me on the shoulder, then brought a large blue eye close to mine.

"Short, shorter, shortest. Three months. You, me, Pellet..."

"Did you just figure that out?" I made room. "Beers, Maestro."

Jimmy was bartending that night. He dug two cold Kever beers out of the case, church-keyed off their tops, and set them in front of us.

Frog threw his cap on the linoleum bar top and said, "Dud Nike-Hercules missiles, Krauts, and cows—what's it mean?"

Frog was a college-op dropout just like me, a drinker, and a gasthaus adventurer. He was bowlegged with a sharp, angled face, which ended in a jutting Hapsburg chin. "Stupidity, dominoes, CIA plots, fear, and inertia—it's too late for 'why' questions."

Frog took a long swallow. He looked at the bottle, then took another swallow. He looked up at the racket near the pinball in time to see Skin kick the Bally into a tilt.

He turned back to me. "Why is it too late?"

"We're not going home in a body bag. That's what the 13th is about. We're alive and bored. We're semi-permanent watchers-from-the-sidelines."

Frog's sharp chin collapsed on his chest. His blue eye groped for meaning. "Almost permanent is right. We're short, Cat. We're going back. A couple days stateside, we won't remember Kever." Frog lit up a cigarette and blew the smoke across the bar towards Jimmy. He looked thoughtful, as if his mind were a thousand miles away. "I wonder what they'll call me when I get back."

That was the precise point when names came up. "Call you?"

"The old name's back there waitin' in the bayou."

"Putrefied, waiting for you to hose off the mud."

Frog grinned, then smiled, as if he were looking at an old dog he liked but had never been able to train. "It's a 'Lester.'"

"At least find another one. Those old names were hooked to the lottery. Did I tell you I won the base Ping-Pong championship?"

"Congratulations," Frog said, without meaning it. "It can't be the same name, can it?"

"Those tribes that bury their names never dig them up. That's the point. Now, contemplate this squat bottle, the confusing Gothic label, the 9% alcohol, and let me tell you about Ping-Pong balls, backspin, and fate."

Frog didn't hear me. Frog was "short." He was getting out. In Frog's case—and mine, I suddenly realized—the timeless sixties hangover was lifting.

Names? It was a very peculiar way to think about getting out. I was born Mathew Hopkins. But in the Midwest, Mathew is too long, except if you want to ape East Coast propriety. I was Matt to most, Stinky to my sister, Big Matt to my father. Matt stayed with me through the four years at Iowa until I met Amy, then I was Matty. Cute, huh?

I was trying to remember Barrett's name—the man who first called me "Cat"—when Frog and I walked out of the canteen. We regarded the sprawling pink stucco building, the heart of the detachment. The North Sea fog penetrated my University of Iowa sweatshirt. We walked towards the barracks. Luftwaffe planes buzzed over storybook farms. Brown and white Fleckvieh cattle shuffled and grunted beyond the cyclone fence.

The barracks was a glowing magnet of lights, which drew the cars in front into perfect rows. I stopped at my white VW fastback. It always reminded me of a poor man's Porsche. There were some books scattered in the rear window ledge, a basketball on the seat, a scattering of papers on the floor. The one I could see was Le Monde. I hated what was happening in the world, but I always had to scratch that itch. I read a couple different papers in a couple different languages just to spite myself.

"Party time," I said.

"Party time?" Frog said, puzzled.

Was Frog going batty on me? He was Frog, Drinker Supreme, disco adventurer. We roamed through the bars of Wilhelmshaven and Bremerhaven together. Once, after a baseball game last summer, we obliterated a case-and-a-half of Kever beer. "No?"

"Party's over."

I frowned then watched Frog shuffle towards the north entrance to the enlisted barracks. I didn't want to go to Kever alone. I jumped the steps of the south entrance, made a pit stop, and whistled down the corridor to my room. Through open doors, I saw guards playing grab-ass, a poker game. Two radio operators, who brought their fondness for hash into the Army, listened to Jefferson Airplane and played head games with their eyes. One of the closed rooms was Bender's. He was one of the two homosexuals on the base. He was always in his room with Grady. Grady would try to sneak out, so no one would suspect they were in there together. But everyone knew.

There were big rooms that slept four, two-man rooms, and a scattering of singles. After the first four months, I got a single. Singles weren't much to look at. It was like a room in the Y. Buffed brown linoleum, hulking armoire, single iron-spring bed, two ratty German-issue chairs. Under the window, next to the front of the bed, was a radiator that belched and coughed and rattled most of the night in winter.

My room was in a post-Christmas, between-inspections mess. I angled around the books scattered on the shiny floor, kicked off my gym shoes, and emptied the rest of my Jack Daniels into a glass. I reached into the armoire, shook the last pack out of the carton, and settled into a chair between armoire and radiator. I lit up, took a sip of whiskey, then ran over the night in my head. The Ping-Pong ball slipped out of the light. It ran along the top of the net like an ironworker along a beam twenty stories up. Then it fell—curled—slowly on Kurt's side.

I went over and over that scene, relishing the win, the claps on the back, the fleeting adulation.

Then I thought of what Frog said. Short, shorter, shortest.

Of course I'd thought about it. Who didn't? It was the one thing that draftees talked about most of the time. Short. Getting out. I guess I had gotten into a rhythm where I hadn't seen the nitty-gritty details of getting out. What was back home, anyway? I made a mental list. Then I realized my list was full of crossed-out entries: Amy married to an Alaskan legislator, parents divorced, the loose gang of friends in Iowa in graduate school or biding their time in the service—those that were still alive. The interesting species of back home, the touchstones—Reich, Leary, Rubin, Ginsberg, the Panthers, the Yippies—were extinct, dissected, indexed, and stored in FBI files.

Mathew Hopkins—Matt, Matty—had been moldering in his grave, just like Frog's "Lester." It didn't look as if I was going to pick up and hose off "Matt" exactly where I'd left him. All I had to work with was "Cat," a local incarnation, a lean draftee who played parlor games.

* * *

The next morning, I shaved, dressed, and walked out of the barracks to an Ostfriesland snowfall. It salted the tile roofs; snow and mud camouflaged the Holsteins over the fence. I followed mud veins through the snow and then wet tracks past the Canteen. I walked down the institutional green and dun corridors to the mess hall in the middle of the pink stucco building. That morning the tables of red-and-white oil, bottles of ketchup, and Red Devil sauce were occupied by guards sleepy from twenty-four-hour duty down range.

"Cat—cool game!" said Lenny, skinny mess sergeant and Vietnam vet. Lenny knew the ropes. He actually wanted to go back to Vietnam. In Nam he was a supply sergeant and made money from everything from toilet paper to eight-track tapes.

"I did it for honor and the U.S. of A."

I grabbed a hard roll, butter, and coffee and followed the

wet tracks through the mess hall. It was like following the track of a huge slug. The hallway was long and dull. Voices came from the end of hallway where Pellet and the top sorted out the paperwork. Captain Osgood and Major Cliff had offices on the right. They didn't come in until nine, just like a regular civilian job. On the left, past the crypto room, was my office where I accounted for Top Secret documents in a large green ledger.

I unlocked the red crypto-room gate then the red door. It was the most secret room in the base, full of codes that could launch the missiles. Why was it red? Wasn't it like a flag? Didn't it say: "Here I am, open me first"?

Inside was gray. Gray filing cabinet, gray creaky Army-issue chair, gray sky out the barred window. And of course there was my gray typewriter, which was more black box than typewriter.

I ate a quick breakfast and got ready to break the low-priority messages. I changed the codes then twirled the plastic rotors. Soon the crazy monkey started making sense of four-letter nonsense syllables. It ground out names of NATO war games, maneuvers, and missile maintenance changes. After-wards, I logged the antique dystopia in my office.

At eleven, I sat back in my Army-issue chair and finessed the daily funk. I smoked a cigarette and drank cold coffee. I stared out the barred window. A deuce-and-a-half rumbled away from the detachment. An extra-duty butt-detail roamed the blotched landscape like an aimless green snow worm.

I was glad to break for lunch. Pellet sat at my table. "Three more months!" Pellet said, between mouthfuls of mashed potatoes. The thick, mud-colored gravy matched eyes scheming under thick brows. He waved his fork at me. "You, me, Frog...all of us."

"I never thought it'd be over."

Pellet finished, lit a cigarette, and took in the noisy sea of fatigues in the mess room. "You know there's nothing back there for these guys."

"Or anyone."

"Look at it how you want. Being short makes me think about the rest."

You are number 87! Congratulations! Throw your life away for two years!

"I'm still thinking about this time-out. How ridiculous it was."

"Or a detour. It's time to think of the future. It's back to business and money."

Pellet already had his MBA. His plan, announced frequently in the canteen, was to get his law degree then become an investment banker for Bear Stearns or Merrill Lynch. "The infernal used car salesman."

Pellet shook his head. "The fallen radical, pining after the good old days."

I hated it when Pellet was right. "You're going back to be the same greedy shit."

"Puss, puss, puss." Pellet's cigarette hissed in the yellow custard, and Pellet hustled up. "I've got to get back—Morning Report madness. Cramer ended up in a polizei drunk tank last night. Might be a court-martial. He was due to leave in a month."

"Fuck."

"A word to the wise."

* * *

At five, I picked up a carton of Camels at the PX and walked down the short hallway to the canteen. It didn't look good. Frog was nursing a coke. "Hey Lester, party time!"

"Got to go down range—duty NCO got sick," said Frog.

I signaled for a beer. "Shit."

Frog gave him me that eye again. "What are you going to be?"

"Is there a portent I'm missing?" I brought my eye close to Frog's blue one. "You don't need to see the chaplain?"

Frog's severe part dropped close to his chest. "I'm not sure. I suppose I'll be Lester Briggs—formerly known as Frog. I'll be what I wanted to be, a civil engineer."

"You got the sign made?"

"They're gonna call me Mr. Briggs. It takes five years to design and produce a new car. It's called planning. We've got to plan. We've got to know what's next."

"It'll come. Don't rush it. It's that stages-of-man thing, the Sphinx questions, the cycles. This is the golden party stage before you go to seed, get fat, and stay in Saturday night. You're going to be Frog and I'm going to be Cat for a few short months. Why not enjoy it?"

Frog picked up his cap, then turned and looked at me with a laser eye. "What about you? You're smart, a good friend, good at parlor games. A year ago you said you wanted to get your doctorate and teach."

"Freelance Hegel explainer, dropout, post-hippie hippie, parlor game guru."

Frog put on his long-billed olive hat with the sergeant decal. "You're not gonna sell out?"

"We haven't already?"

"You are depressing."

A deuce-and-a-half appeared like Dracula's coach, and Frog went away to polish the dud nukes. The canteen was tired that night. Beyond the junk heap pinball, stacks of Kever leaned as if they were going to collapse out of boredom. A couple draftees, Worm and Crab—did we all have weird names?—moved bottles of Kever in ritual circles on the bar top.

I should have left, except I had another bottle. Then another. I got an inkling of the problem. I had been so detached from reality, so bored for so long, I didn't know what I was going to do.

I felt better when I left the canteen. The sky that afternoon had been dark. Flakes of snow drifted through the lights. I followed the hardening trail back to the barracks.

I stopped at my car. Kever and its discos?

Inertia led to my room. I picked up the Manchester Guardian and the Frankfurter Allgemeine, which the courier had dropped near the front door. I took a long leak in the bathroom, then I went back to a room stuffed with garbage and an armoire full of booze.

I made a drink of vodka and tomato juice, lit a cigarette, and read the news. The European newspapers gave me perspective but no solace. Eurodollars, Cold War maneuvering, the Kent State photo, the body bag count. The war, which trapped me and Frog and Pellet, ground on like a steamroller. The war had been banal for so long it had become like breakfast or morning coffee.

I threw the papers on the floor. I made another drink. That's when I saw my Backhome drawer. I took out the drawer and emptied it on the bed.

I sorted letters and photos. Airmail envelope, enclosed photo. Amy, ex-lover. The Mendenhall glacier rose behind her cliff-like. We went to Alaska together. Against the backdrop of the war, the draft, we planned our family. Two kids named after grandparents. We'd go back to graduate school. I would find a teaching job; she would be a librarian. We were going to live in a university town, either Madison or Iowa City. Her husband took the photo. I don't know why she sent it. I wadded up the photo and banked it off the bookcase into the wastebasket for two.

A Polaroid taken after a march the pigs broke up. I was bearded, serious, hopeful, my arm clutching the jacket of someone I didn't know. I read the back, "Matt and Dave, Chicago." I remembered. Dave. Political science. He was going to be a prof. Killed in Vietnam. John Macky told me it was a Bouncing Betty, the ones that bounce into the air then spray needle-like shards into everything living in a twenty-foot radius.

Keeper.

Graduation photo. Brow bursting with hope. My parents, John and Joan Hopkins, sat on either side of my sister. They barely glanced at each other, but then they were separated, and a few months later divorced. In a sense I would be starting over. And that was always a good thing. Right?

Conditional keeper.

Induction notice. Bank, basket.

Where had all the flowers gone? Where was my golden

era, so pregnant, so bursting with newness? Where were the songs, the reinvention of intimacy, the heroism?

Basket. Keeper. Basket.

At ten, I put on jeans, work shirt, thick socks, and boots. I slung my heaviest Army jacket over my shoulder. The corridor was curiously quiet, the doors shut. From the barracks door, the night seemed endless. The cows moved in slow motion across the fence. The lights from headquarters spread like butter over the patchy snow.

A few minutes later, I drove slowly past the stubble of buildings. The lights in the rec room were still on. Two GIs in white undershirts played Ping-Pong under the stretch of eyeshade lights. I veered along the arc away from the base. A few moments later I raced past a shivering German sentry, who watched me with envious eyes. I gunned the VW between the severe hedges of the road to Kever. In the distance, barren trees stretched spindly branches into the darkness. The trees made me feel isolated, as if I had been truly cut off from my friends, my past, my era.

Kever, Kever. Kevel? Dever? One day I'd try to remember the name and wouldn't.

Kaiser Gasthaus. I ordered a rum-and-coke and lit up. The Volk peered at me over their bratwurst, shish kebob, and finger-thick fries. I wanted to yell, to break them out of their stolid complacency. They thought I was a drunk Amerikanisch Soldat. No, I was the radical Matt. No, I was the soft domestic Matty. No, I was Cat.

I stubbed out my cigarette, finished my drink, and stumbled outside.

I headed towards Tapitas, a local disco. I followed the cone of my breath down the narrow streets, slipping over quaint cobblestones. A few minutes later I was in Tapitas listening to Beach Boys and polkas, mesmerized by a Roaring 20's globe, which lanced balls of light in the corners and teased rainbows out of my rum-and-coke.

I tried to pick up a stocky Fraulein with spun curls. She turned away. I grabbed her shoulder. A young German in an ill-fitting black suit stood in front of me. He had a retro-Elvis duck cut. His eyes were serious, his hands in fists.

"Sorry, sorry. Entshuldegin, bitte." He relaxed. They both stared at me.

I shrugged, killed my drink, and stumbled outside.

The Village Square was a white bowl with boot marks, sled tracks, and icy trenches as if giant fingers had dragged through the snow. Two beetleboys in caps and mufflers threw snow, which exploded like firecrackers and floated in the air. I didn't feel the cold. The few flakes that drifted through the town glow tickled my hands.

I kicked a piece of ice down the longest trench and watched it skitter down the bumpy, slick path. Images flickered in and out of focus. Photos, an airmail letter, a graduation pin.

Mathew, Matt, Matty, Cat.

Those trenches looked slick. You'd never reach the bottom in one piece, unless you were especially good on your feet. Unless you were a cat. Cats always landed on their paws.

I turned away from the trenches, then turned back. Sometimes drunks are prescient. They figure the world out. The problem is that either they don't remember the next day, or there never is a next day. I was at a cusp. I was standing before an empty Village Square in the middle of nowhere. I knew, knew the way a drunk knows, that I would find an answer, the answer, at the end of the night. And I was going to start with those trenches.

I walked over to the longest one. I zipped up my jacket. I posed on the hill like a diver and pushed off. Halfway down I hit something and the sky became a bowl, a cap with little white holes, a thousand Ping-Pong balls stuck in the sky. I was Cat. I always landed on my feet. I did a quaint dance, my arms raised, as if I were imploring the sky. Gravity nudged me forward.

I was surprised I didn't land on my feet. I threw out my hands. My head bounced on the ice. I was stunned that I wasn't standing up. It seemed wrong. Then teardrops of blood made dull mosaics on the ice under my nose. I got up and lurched up the hill. Flakes drifted through the disco's red glow. I stumbled past leaning walls. I held onto a tree, then the next. I fell. I was sober enough to know I couldn't drive. I steadied myself on the tree and hauled myself up.

"Wo ist mein Name?" I yelled into a huddle of blank faces outside a gasthause.

"Sie sind Trinker," said a thick voice.

"Er ist baüfallig," said another, shaking his head.

"Wo ist mein Name?" I dug under the snow. It was somewhere close, near my chest. I blew on the glass of a closed café. I wrote "Cat" on its gray surface.

I yelled into webs of branches. I was being the ugly American. I was making a fool of myself. Blood dripped randomly from my face. Faces disappeared into yellow hallways. A German sign pointed up, down, sideways. The topsy-turvy world stretched to the edge of the night.

"Gott in Himmel! Ich muss ein Trink haben," I yelled into a heavy German face.

"Nein," said the stout bartender, pointing at my front. The blood made dark stains on the olive-green Army jacket. "Polizei."

"Nein. Nicht polizei."

I stumbled on for a block. Then I felt, rather than heard it. A black-and-white polizei van sped towards me. I remembered what Pellet said.

Stockade. Court martial.

I stumbled down an alley, then another. The siren was closer, then farther away.

I was on a small street, poorly lit, with small, neat houses.

I spelled the name on the sign. Dr. K-R-O-G-E-R.

I rang the bell. A few minutes later, a heavy man in striped pajamas opened the door. Behind him, a squeaky voice said "Was ist? Was ist? Was ist?

"Ich bin Amerikanish. Mein Name ist kaput."

He shook his head as if I'd mangled German, not my face. "Not your name, your nose."

"You speak English. Please don't call the police. I have money."

I dug in my pockets and dollars fell to the floor. They lay on the floor like crumpled leaves. "Sorry. Sorry." I bent, spread my arms, and made a pile of dollars. I looked up at Dr. Kroger.

He shook his head, as if I were a backward child. "Come with me."

I stuffed dollars in my jacket and stumbled after him. He had a small office in the house. A few minutes later I sat on the edge of a white table.

"Who are you?" said Dr. Kroger.

I found my Army ID and gave it to him.

"You are Mathew Hopkins. It's a good name."

"Yes."

"Lie back."

I lay back. Thick fingers pushed my nose this way and that. Then he stuffed it with a mile-long piece of gauze.

"You need stitches," said Dr. Kroger. "Above the eye and across the bridge of the nose."

I wasn't in any shape to contradict him. But I wondered: What will I look like? Would anyone recognize me?

Dr. Kroger's thick fingers sewed around my eye like knitting needles. Then he sewed over the bridge of my nose. It felt for a moment that I was an old doll and Dr. Kroger was sewing me back together.

I spoke into the flicking fingers. "I am Mathew Hopkins."

Kroger's face was a frozen lump. "Yes you are."

After Dr. Kroger finished, I knew he had to make a choice. He looked at me for what seemed a long time, shrugged. "I'll call a cab. You have enough money."

"I have to pay you."

"Later. If you remember."

I didn't want to leave his house. I felt safe, secure. Outside was winter. I'd be alone. I'd be Cat again. A cab appeared at his door. I turned and saw him standing there, pulling his pajamas together against the cold. "I'm sorry. Thank you. Thank you."

He shrugged.

I stumbled down the stairs and almost fell. I showed the cab driver my money. When I shut the door, he sped off towards the base.

I don't remember the ride. Doors opened and slammed. Lights turned on and off. I rolled along an edge, faceless and nameless. I dropped into a bed of letters, envelopes, and photos.

***

I woke up with the sun and a blinding headache. My room was a wasteland of letters, photos, and newspapers. I got my towel, soap, and shampoo and walked zombie-like to the shower. I tried to keep the water away from my face. I rubbed the mirror over the sink and stared at black eyes, a stitched half-moon near the bridge of my nose, and packed nostrils with a single thread dropping from the right nostril.

I walked my battered head back to my room, dressed, and gingerly put on my cap. Outside, I stared down, shielding my head from the light. After a few seconds, I looked up. The sun shone. Icicles dripped slowly from the edge of the slanted roof. Over the cyclone fence, brown and white cattle moved sluggishly through mud and snow clumps.

I shut the door of the barracks, walked through the parking lot, and soon walked carefully over the icy path snaking towards headquarters. As I walked, I reconstructed the night, the non-stop drinking, the thuggish behavior in Tapitas, the long icy trough, the bowl of the starry night sky, the stupid push-off, and my blood making mosaics on the dark ice. Dr. Kroger. The cab ride.

As for the night, I'd remember the outlines, a few high points. Likely my wager with the icy slope. Maybe Dr. Kroger.

I suppose most significant times of my life would be like that: half-remembered.

The night made me know one thing clearly.

Cat Hopkins was short.

TRASH PAD

There is a subset of humanity which lives for bars. They may be lawyers, bankers, programmers, construction workers, or shoe repairmen. They may have kids and wives or husbands or just someone else, but the climax of their day is when they walk through the welcoming doors of a bar and are greeted like lost brothers even though they were there the night before doing exactly the same thing.

There are thousands of ways the life of the bar has been analyzed through the centuries, but few can doubt the pump and colors and fleeting happiness of such a life. It is, of course, worse in college towns like Iowa City, the Harvard of Interstate 80, home to the Writer's Workshop and also home to so many bars the inhabitants can't count them anymore.

Sam Perkin was a bar guy. He was an Irish redhead, a befreckled, impish, charming redhead with a gift for talking and a thirst for booze and women. His favorite bar was Pete's, one of the last old bars in the city, a bar with old wood, an old back bar of volute pillars and wreath scrolls, etched mirrors. As you came in, there was a Bally pinball and in back an antediluvian juke box. The bar still had pickled eggs and bratwurst, and the clientele could get drunk and pass out in their booths, at least for a while. It was a bar where the owner, although he had an au courant oxymoronic "drug-free zone" poster displayed in back of the bar, wouldn't know a joint from a vial of crack if they were tested and labeled. The owner was Pete Healy, another Irishman. When Sam finished his MA and graduated, Pete had just thrown three students out of the apartment upstairs, and Sam took it over. It was a double whammy for Sammy. He not only spent his nights in Pete's, he lived there too.

But Sam had to work to play, and he did it as a programmer for GLM, a mutant national testing enterprise spreading over four acres north of the city. Sam was bright and liked solving problems—normally, but lately he was working on a new program that was becoming his nemesis.

That day he had worked hard on it. It was tortuous. The logic, which he had designed himself, impenetrable. It was day life, he thought sourly; we design mazes for ourselves we can't figure out. Finally, he looked at the lines of code on the programming sheet with their indented procedures and commands and branches, crumpled up the sheet, and tossed it the green wastebasket. He raised himself in a semi-crouch and looked over the partition of his cube like the storied cube prairie dog.

He shouldn't have done that. It was like waving a red flag in the room. Come see Sam; he's waving his head again. But the other prairie dogs, especially his manager, were off tending their own mazes. He ducked down and closed his project. The wastebasket accused him: he'd just thrown away the changes he'd sweated over for all day.

Good, he thought as he got his windbreaker and headed to the parking lot. Excellent. But why was it good? It just felt good, as if he'd struck a blow against an insane order. Maybe it felt good because he was letting go. In the last week, he'd felt the rope tying him to his city slipping through his hands. He would quit his job and leave. He could find another Pete's, couldn't he? He thought about that as he wedged his

35

lean frame into his Triumph Spitfire and aimed it towards the city.

Before he knew it, he was in a traffic jam. A traffic jam in Iowa City? He'd watched the city become the southern terminus of a Cedar Rapids/IC sprawl cinched up with new malls, stores, cars, and concrete. What was that Aborigine saying about everything spinning out of control? Or was it Yeats and his gyre?

He was so wrapped up in his musing that he almost missed the soft fall colors and turning leaves. Yesterday it was summery, today nippy. Splotches of sun made the pastures of the few farms that were left a crazy-quilt of gold and brown.

He would miss the fall and that drive and all the rest.

He parked on Iowa Avenue, and a few minutes later he walked into Pete's. Iowa City used to have character, but Pete's was the only place in Iowa City which felt like the old days.

Pete's was smoky, dark, cavernous, and loud and full. "Hey guys," he said to the Barley brothers and their girlfriends, who were banging on the Bally pinball to the left of the door. "Weren't you here last night?"

"And we'll be here tomorrow," said Tom, the oldest brother.

He watched the shiny ball bouncing through its maze and ricocheting off bumpers. "Later."

He sat at the stool nearest the door and waited for Tim, the bartender. "Tim, a short one," he said, when Tim came over.

"You got it, big guy. Is it party time?"
"Maybe next week."

"You don't sound yourself tonight. What's up? Tell Tim."

"Mazes, depression, and life. I'm not myself. Maybe I just need a good drunk."

"Sounds chronic. Just tell me about the next party; I'll bring a bottle of Jameson."

He loved Pete's. He loved living above a bar. He loved parties and lots of intelligent people acting like morons. He liked the dark side of life, he'd decided, when he wanted to justify it. And he liked the sex. Meet, drink, and come up to my parlor said the spider to the fly. It was almost a ritual, and he had a rep. Sometimes it bothered him. The parties had become white noise, the gals more trouble than the chase, and he'd lost control of his apartment months ago. Everyone knew where his spare key was. He'd found cigarettes smoldering in his ashtrays and stray people wandering around his bedroom. Last week a friend of a friend, a singer in a C&W band, was taking a bath when he came in.

While Tim got him his beer, he stared at his reflection in the bar mirror. The Irish imp was there, but the eyes were sardonic. He felt like an alien.

Maybe it was time to get into the night. He picked up his beer and walked towards the pool table in back.

It was crowded as usual. Students scraped glasses across marble table tops in the booths, and groups of two and three hashed their day to pieces in the aisle and at the bar. There was the steady drone of voices, and he greeted faces whose voices he'd already picked out. Hi Tim, Goldie, and Karl. Hi John and Sandy.

"Hi Pat, Mindy." He was casual and leaned against the top of the booth. Pat was one of his pool partners and

Mindy was, well, she was a lover when Pat wasn't around, a blond-haired, kinda round addition to Sam's Rumpus Room. They had long chats afterwards, usually about getting caught. It added spice, but he didn't know what he'd do if Pat appeared in his bedroom doorway one day, hurt and accusing or pissed.

He smiled and played a game of double entendre with Mindy until he saw they were dressed up. "Playing pool, Pat?"

"Not tonight," said Pat.

"We're going to Hancher. The ballet," said Mindy.

"It's good to get away sometimes," Sam said.

"You should try it yourself," said Pat. "You're a fixture."

"We all want stability," Sam said.

"There has to be more, n'est-ce pas?" said Mindy.

It was one of Pete's favorite topics, the outside world and how it reinforced Pete's. "I suppose there is. I'm for pool."

"Stay out of trouble," said Mindy. Translation: stay away from other women, you jerk.

"Enjoy the ballet, my friends."

At the far end of the bar, the pool table was like the light of a hidden treasure. He hunkered down on the edge of the bar and watched Morris and Rob miss shots. They were terrible pool players and their games lasted an eternity. He saw a thin figure detach itself from the wall.

He hadn't seen Kenny Margolis and he didn't want to see him. Kenny was an anorexic sociology student—a scheming Brecht with bug eyes and a butch haircut. A few months ago, he'd let Kenny use his apartment for a tryst, and Kenny and his trystee had camped in his apartment for a week.

"My favorite redhead," Kenny said, as he took the stool on his left and hovered close to his shoulder. "I'm glad you're here. I've got a tiny problem with Cindy."

"You'll always have a problem with Cindy."

"You think she'd understand what 'open' marriage meant," Kenny sighed.

"Maybe she thinks it means 'closed.'"

"As if you care. So I've got this new friend and what I want to ask is—"

"If you can borrow my apartment for a year. The answer is no way."

"You don't understand. I'll pay you fifty bucks and buy all your beer—"

"You're an albatross, not a sociologist. Don't talk to me."

Kenny's Adam's apple bobbed up and down like a yo-yo: "Everyone uses your apartment," said Kenny. "You're what we call a 'facilitator' in transaction theory."

He looked at Kenny. "The facility is fermé. Entritt verboten. Closed."

"We'll talk after my game," said Kenny before he went back to his spot on the wall.

Morris came out of the bathroom with quaaluded glass eyes, and Rob went outside to smoke a joint. That should have been good news pool-wise, but the list for the table was still as long as his arm, and he knew Kenny would bug him all night. He stubbed out his cigarette and was wondering what to do when Tim threw him an envelope.

"What's this?"

"Jimmy gave it to me when my shift started."

He opened the envelope and spread out the letter. The

words were spaced close together in tiny elegant lines. He read: "Sorry about the apartment. Might see you later. Mary." Mary? Mary was usually in the big booth next to the pool table. She wasn't there now.

He made new circles on the envelope with his glass, looked around once more at the pool table list, finished his beer and decided to find out what "sorry about the apartment" meant.

"Leaving so soon?" said Tim.

"I'll be back." Two doors later, he was climbing the steps with their worn rubber protectors and blinking against the light which hung twenty feet from the sloping ceiling. Those tacky steps always reminded him of The Prince and the Pauper, about someone sneaking into a deserted alley, opening a worn door, then stepping into a palace, or something like a palace. He felt like that about his apartment. It was tacky outside and you could hear the yells from the bar, but he liked what was inside. It was a gem, cozy with hanging plants, throw rugs, stuffed sofas, and Gauguin prints.

Then again, it looked like the palace doors were open for business. He pushed his door open the rest of the way and saw a trash pad: the fat yellow sofa pillows lay on the floor like dead and bloated fish, an ashtray had landed in his over-stuffed reading chair, and his floor lamp slanted across the doorway, blocking off the bedroom.

He closed his eyes. He shook his head then opened them again. It was still there, his trash pad. It looked like someone had staged a demolition derby. He sighed, picked up his sofa cushions, and threw them back on the sofa. Then he toured his apartment like the Red Cross after a disaster. The fading September light, which crawled past the lamp and up the east wall, showed him the cracked aquarium and its spiky cactus were OK. The walk-in kitchen was as good as it could be. The fridge looked OK and his wine and beer were untouched.

He came back into the living room and checked out the bedroom from the doorway. The bedroom needed help. The Rex begonia had suffered a hit, and the dirt from its smashed pot fanned out in an alluvial plain. The brown spines of a few books and loose pages spread over to the windows. His jade plant was down and the leaves scattered like green fingers.

He picked up the lamp and put it where it was supposed to be, then checked out the undraped window. It was open, which was not a good sign. He looked out over the tarry roofs and a sun fading off the Old Capitol dome to see if anyone was out there and decided they weren't.

It could have been a lot worse. He picked up a cigarette from a pack next to the broken pot and sat on his unmade bed, trying to figure out what had happened and couldn't come close. There were a lot of women who had been through there. Was it possible one got really pissed and decided to get back? But what did that have to do with Mary?

He put out his cigarette and was about to start cleaning when he heard a knock on the door and the door open and close. A few seconds later Mary Connor stepped through the doorway and stared at him from the foot of the bed. Her ponytail was gone and a mop of black hair hung over her eyes. Mary, usually the coy ingénue, looked like a waif in a schlock-shop painting. Her hand plucked nervously at the threads of a missing button on her faded work shirt.

"So what happened?"

"Did you get my note?" said Mary.

"And?"

"It'll be funny tomorrow," she said. She stroked his sheets and then sat down on the bed next to him; then she picked a cigarette out of the pack on the floor and lit it. "George thought you and I had slept together," she said. She looked at him meaningfully as if that meant something.

"Shit." Mary and George were a pool table item. While George played pool, Mary drank pints that were too big for her hands and read books in the glow from the pool table. Last week, he'd spent a night listening to Mary brag about her gay, bi, and straight escapades. He'd thought at the time: he was Don Juan and she was mixed-up Salome. They would make an earth-splitting item, except he didn't like her. Then there was George. He didn't want too many outraged husbands and boyfriends writing his name at the top of their hate list. "But we haven't come close."

"I didn't tell him," she said, tearing out the threads and letting them flutter to the floor.

"You didn't tell him we haven't?"

"I tell him everything. He thought I was keeping you a secret."

"Why not lie?"

"If I'd lied it would have been worse."

"I'm missing a beat." He pointed his forefinger at his pots on the floor and his books.

"You seem such a pushover, but you're always skipping from one to another, like a child who can't make up his mind."

"Maybe I can't make up my mind."

"Maybe you should."

"Maybe you should."

"I know, I know. I think if I stop, then it's over."

He stared out the open window. The darkening light was leaving the soft outlines of telephone poles and TV antennas sticking into the sky over the tar roof. The Old Capitol Dome looked tarnished. He looked at the jade leaves on the floor; they still looked like disembodied fingers. He got up and picked his way through the rubble and came back with half a bottle of Medoc and two glasses. Mary slipped out of her Birkenstocks and tucked her feet underneath her.

"Why come here?"

"George wanted to talk to you. When you weren't here, he got mad and chased me through here." Mary paused, then said: "I shouldn't tell you, but George finally calmed down and we made love right here." She patted his sheets. "You can see everything from out on the roof—you don't have any curtains!" A smugness played in a streak of hair on Mary's upper lip, as if she were proud she had another tale for the pool table crowd.

"Where is he now?"

"We've had problems before, but it's never gone this far," Mary said, ignoring him.

"I should leave town," he said, ignoring Mary.

"We can't be together anymore, but a crazy thing happens—like this—and we end up back together. It's OK for a while, but then it gets old again." She looked sheepish and pulled at her hair. "I didn't mean for this to happen, but I can't control it after a certain point."

He lit two more cigarettes. The flame shadowed Mary's bruised face and went out in her swollen eyes. They smoked in silence. He'd never looked at Mary before. He'd wondered what she'd be like in bed—a small soft shadow under his lean body. She'd be like the Cheshire Cat.

43

Mary gave him her cigarette and he put it out. Her hands were larger than he'd thought, the fingers soft and fingernails dirty. Then she looked at him and, for a moment, looked forlorn and lost again. They had definitely hooked into a lost-souls night. She leaned towards him and rested her head on his shoulder. "You don't mind if I step out of character, do you?"

"Are you stepping out of character or just trying a new one?"

"I don't know."

"It doesn't matter."

"Would it be strange if I stayed here tonight? Even though we made up, George still feels guilty." Her small voice came out of his shoulder. The faint light of sunset was fading into darkness. It didn't look like he'd get on the road that night. "Tell George I'm leaving and you're staying."

"Are you leaving?"

"It's time to go."

"Just when I'm starting to like you."

He finally understood: he'd said it was time to let go, but he hadn't believed it until he'd seen his trash pad. Mary had jump-started his trip.

He wasn't sure what would happen that night. After another half bottle of wine, he still didn't know. The moon shone through his curtainless windows and washed over the scattered plants and the scattered pages of his books.

Mary was silent, then he knew she was staring at him, then he felt her hand on his, then her mouth on his own.

It looked like one for the road.

THE RUG

It all started months ago.

I, Dante Meno, am a short, typically swarthy Italian with thick curly black hair and lambent brown eyes. George Fair, my boss in title only, is a tall, pale WASP with hunched shoulders and a retiring manner. We were Lewis and Clark, Mutt and Jeff, Abbot and Costello.

George and I work in New York City in Tribeca on the eighth floor of a drab building where we share space with twenty other New York State auditors. Let's clear this up right away: we have sinecures. The civil service is a fortress protected by a thick wall with barbed wire wound like springs across the top and shards of glass embedded in the cement. We cannot be fired and venture into the real world only to retire. Our salaries, modest though they are, are deposited like clockwork in our checking accounts. When we have to, we protect our jobs with well-placed and well-timed memos; or, we do a few sheets of general ledger to keep the resident floor manager, Growber, and Cummings, his boss on the ninth floor, and his boss in Albany, at bay. Our work day is spent following the Yankees, Jets, or Knicks, reading romances, writing short stories, or polishing nails. George—diffident and self-deprecating, a Mr. Uriah Heep without unction—writes unpublishable poetry and does the Times crossword. I tried to write, once, but have given up my pretensions for mysteries. I read a lot of mysteries and in the evening talk plots and formulas in the Cave, my favorite Greenwich Village bar.

One day George's hair started falling.

"Tough," I told Barbara, my sometimes girlfriend, a buyer for Macy's. "It's the march of time."

"You could be sympathetic," said Barbara.

"He already looks like a praying mantis. It's nature having a little fun."

If nature was making jokes, George wasn't laughing.

I didn't notice much at first, but when I glanced in his direction, I saw hesitation. I saw his pencil stop over a blank page. He spent hours in the bathroom, I suppose, to see if anything had fallen in the last hour. Curious, I thought; then I went back to Ross Macdonald. I noticed other changes. George started keeping a comb by his side a little like a six-shooter. He got into parts. One day it was the "swept-up" look, the next the "swept-over" look, the part slowly descending towards the ear or neck. The parts didn't last long. The slightest puff of air made the covering hair raise and settle slowly back over his dome.

The rest of us, especially Millie, an aspiring actress, and Bennett, English and a soccer obsessive, who sits directly across from me, joked about George's dilemma. We shared secret glances and hid smirks. Even Growber got into the act and chuckled over George's struggle.

George did struggle. After combs and parts came potions and lotions. He tried Rogaine. He gobbled a new pill from Pfizer which opened blocked pores and untangled hair. His hair fell faster. Magazines like Manly Hair or Men and Hair sprouted between piles of auditing forms and scribbles of poetry. We all guessed it was time for more radical measures, but what were they? Weaving? Hair Club for Men? One day George rolled up his pants and looked at his legs. What was that? Would we soon salute corn rows from George's nether regions?

Then George was quiet. It was July. It was vacation time. Bennett was visiting family in England, and Millie had taken a week off to act in The Taming of the Shrew off-Broadway. We had a skeleton crew which included George and me. George seemed too composed, his image dark against the white, heavy sky in his window. Had he accepted his fate? Was he going to be Yul Brynner? The answer was no. He went to the bathroom and an hour later appeared with the rug, a discolored mop cured in sallow yellow turpentine, perched on his head.

I had to do something; the rug was an aesthetic disaster. I took George to our favorite Greek diner for lunch. It was in the Western Union building on Hudson Street. I had ravioli, George a BLT. "It's time, Dante," said George between bites. "Pythagoras, the Cycle of Life. I've tried to grasp a certain ineffability in my poetry, but I've failed." George placed his BLT on his plate and was silent for a moment, as if what he'd said were finally sinking in.

"It's the journey that's important, George. Don't get distracted."

"A few months ago," George continued, "I was happy. I would grow old and write obscure poetry. I would go to the same deli and get the same pastrami sandwich every day."

I looked at his hands—they were long, smooth, and large at the fingertips, vulnerable and sensitive—he was a poet. "What could be more heroic," I said, "than trying to express the chords of nature or the doomed yearning of man to soar beyond his earthly fate?"

"I know, I know. I can't help it; it's change or die."

Change or die?

"Just because you're losing a little hair?"

"I am?"

Do people who lose hair develop a nictitating membrane over their intelligence? Didn't George know he was wearing a rug? "Let's back up. You've been losing hair for months. You've tried twenty different cures. Right now you're wearing a toupée, a topper, a hairpiece, a rug. It looks like a mop that's been dragged through a barber shop."

George gave me a weak necrotic smile. "Is it that obvious?"

"It's a blue light special. It's like a highway patrol light. It sticks out like that girl with the giant thumb in Even Cowgirls Get the Blues. I can't take my eyes off it."

George was quiet; then he lowered his eyes. "It makes me feel younger."

And that was that.

That evening, Barbara and I went to House of Cards at the Quad. I loved it. It was the perfect mystery. Where is the pea? Afterwards we went to the Cave but instead of House of Cards, the topic was George's rug.

"He's acting like a fool. But what business is it of mine?"

"I feel sorry for him. I suppose I'd do the same."

"Women don't go bald."

"Some do. Then if you have chemo..."

"Forget George's rug. Let's have another round and I'll let you play with Pollywog."

"You mean play with you. OK, Dante, ply me with liquor."

And I did, and we did, and she did play with Pollywog, my Siamese.

But George's rug had anchored itself like a mast in spiritual space. I tried to go about my business. I reread all of Le Carré and talked over Cold War double-crosses in the Cave. I fought with and bedded Barbara. I straightened my ever-growing library of three thousand mysteries. I played catch-the-swinging-mouse with Pollywog. Things seemed normal, but even then, early on, I felt a flicker of doom, a nagging sense that the rug was going to cause trouble.

At work, I watched George pen his poetry and do his crosswords. If the rug made him happy, he didn't show it. There was a hint of misery about George which I saw but didn't understand.

I was right; the rug was a symptom. A few weeks after the rug made its appearance, George enlisted in a dating service. He started wearing suits to work and making calls during the day. Dating was a bust at first, but then he met Beryl Matson. Beryl was fortyish, near George's age, and had sharp brown eyes, tough brown curls, a jutting nose, a respectable job on Wall Street, and a failing for failing poets. I started getting the picture. "Failed poet" was not a catchy epitaph. George was making a late dash at the gold ring.

As for Beryl, she became a big part of George's last try at what I can only call middle-class mediocrity. He whispered phone calls to her. They went to movies and they did dinner. Somewhere in their dating game, they fell into bed and George found a spring in his step.

"You could use a spring too," said Barbara with little provocation.

"What about my spring?"

"Not spring, but something more solid. You're in a holding pattern, Dante. You have everything lined up perfectly. Me, your mysteries, your job. It feels like tundra, frozen and dead."

"That's bad?"

"You've traded your soul for habit."

"I never had a soul in the first place."

It started me thinking nonetheless. Perhaps my life had become too patterned, too dead. Is that bad? Don't we all want things to stay the same? If nothing else, it was the first time George's rug messed with my life. It wasn't the last.

Beryl and George, George and Beryl. Did he take his rug off before they did it? What did she really think of it? Was she discreet? I gave up Le Carré for watching George. I listened in to phone calls. I heard him fight with Beryl. Fight? Pre-rug, George couldn't fight with a paperboy.

Homeostasis. George's life reached a new accommodation, and everyone he worked with accepted it. His rug, Beryl, a spring in his step. I supposed it was good for George and left it at that, except George's little drama entered a new stage when Growber tacked a job announcement on the bulletin board. George was on it like a flash. What? My George? The George who wrote poetry and did the Times crossword? That noon I sauntered over and read the posting. It was a supervisor slot, Grade 23. That slot would give George four other Dantes, an extra five thousand a year, and would boost him up to the ninth floor. He had to convince Growber to recommend him then convince Cummings on the ninth floor that he was the man for the job.

I tried to make George see reason at Joe's in the Village.

George seemed to have latched on to "change" as his personal mantra. "I am going to get that Grade 23 slot. I know it."

"This fast-track business has gone to your head." His rug shifted. "Metaphorically, of course."

A wan smile disturbed George's face. "I have no doubt that soon I'll be headed up to the ninth floor or even to Albany. Of course, I'd have to figure that out with Beryl."

"Naturally."

"And I will have to change a few things at work."

"What things?"

"I'm not sure. But if I'm going to get that job, things have to change."

I left it at that; but what was George going to change? The next day, I noticed the crosswords were gone along with the poetry—he hadn't written with any diligence for months anyway. On the other hand, George had a résumé a high schooler would be ashamed of. George had as much chance of winning the lottery as getting that Grade 23 slot; but then it was civil service.

I didn't think much of George's ambition until he wrote his letter. The letter was about morale on the eighth floor, copies to Growber and Cummings. It was about Millie and Bennett and me and the rest of us. George had turned and he kept turning.

Then he started working.

Then he started on me.

"Dante, I'd like to see you," George mumbled as he squinted at a paper on his desk.

I looked up from an old edition of Conan Doyle, which I'd hidden under a pile of auditing forms. I regarded George: what was up?

I marked my place, pulled auditing forms over it, and got up from my desk. On my right, extending down a narrow corridor to the back stairs, Millie, Bennett, and ranks of auditors, QA, and support staff popped up their heads like gophers.

I walked across the shiny floor to George's desk. George's voice had assumed a false edge of command which, as I approached his desk, George tried to efface with a weak smile. The stares of my compatriots weighed on my back.

I stood in front of George's desk, rocked on my heels, rumpled my curly hair, flicked an imaginary piece of dust off his desk, and kicked off our dialogue. "George."

I looked down at George and instead of taking in the whole of his lean visage, my eyes were drawn like magnets to the top of his head and a hairpiece that seemed slightly askew.

George pyramided his hands and looked directly into my eyes. "Dante, it's been so long anyone's worked in this team, people have forgotten how. But I'm going to change that."

"Anyone? People? We're a team of two, George. Where is the rest of your battalion?"

"That's not the point." George's eyes bored into mine, as if by force of will he was going to break the lock my eyes had on his rug. And I tried again—I wasn't trying to bait George. I stared at Hudson Street and watched people leaving the Western Union building. I watched gladiolus being picked out in the flower shop on the corner and the door of the Greek restaurant opening and closing, hoping that when I returned to George, I could look him dead in the eyes. I couldn't. I was trapped, again, by the shiny brown fibers perched askew on George's head.

I closed my eyes as if I were thinking and said, "I am willing to do anything to make this the auditing team in the State of New York. You know that."

Did he? I was Dante, sinecurist, protector of my slot, isolationist. "Yes, well, of course. It's not a question of this thing or that thing. It is a question of adopting a stance. It's not the doing but the framework and the attitude. When that's in place, the rest follows."

"Great. If you want to—have to—improve it, I'm ready."

"I knew you'd say that. But saying and doing are two separate things." George looked at me; I stared at his rug. "Could I ask you to do something else, right now?"

"Of course."

"Stop staring at my head!"

"Was I?" I said while trying to look in George's eyes.

"You know you were!"

"I have an observation," I said, warming up.

"Make it brief; I have a lot of work today."

George wanted our tête-à-toupée to end, but he'd passed his testiness to me like a baton in a relay. "It involves asking why I stare. The answer should be obvious to the most obscure poet. You're wearing a rug that's plastered oddly on your head."

A weak smile disturbed George's face. "Thank you for

your uninformed opinion. Now back to work!" George said "work" loudly so that Growber could hear it.

Papers rustled behind me as I walked to my desk. I scattered an extra layer of auditing forms over my desk and tried to resume The Sign of the Four. I couldn't.

The whole mess came up as usual with Barbara, like a mantra. "It's not about a rug; it's about aging, women, sex, and the whole ball of wax," I said.

Barbara took a sip of her drink and stared past the rim at me. "And how that messes with your mysteries and Dante keeping his little corner all swept and tidy. And what's wrong with women?"

"Let's leave my mysteries out of this—"

"Dante, this is about you, not George. George is trying to change; you're not."

"I'm happy in my backwater."

"You're hopeless. Maybe you should find another more comatose frog for your pond."

I knew Barbara didn't mean it, but maybe she did. How did that happen? Maybe I did have to find someone else to share it. But I had another problem, a bigger problem, the problem of whether George would make it and whether my mysteries would go bye-bye.

That's when I got drawn into George's quest in earnest. George was forcing my hand and, if he got that job, what would happen to me? It was more than protecting my job. I was protecting a lifestyle.

It was time to do something concrete, but what? I talked to Millie and Bennett. They had already been called into Growber's office where, because of George's note about laxness on our floor, their work habits were raked over the coals. Millie talked about quitting, Bennett about going back to England. Auditing forms with yellow Post-It notes appeared on my desk with "Immediate" inscribed on them and underlined.

After mulling over my options one night, I zeroed in on my goal. In order to preserve the status quo, I had to torpedo George's chances of getting that Grade 23 slot. It's odd how things work out. Barbara, almost mystically, called it "synchronicity." I think it has more to do with knowing your goal and unconsciously filtering out those things that don't help you. What's left assembles itself in a kind of scheme, not unlike most mysteries.

And so it was with my goal. One day I wandered into Growber's office and asked him about the Grade 23 slot. Growber didn't trust any of us, although he ran his own real estate business from his office. He asked me what I thought of it. I told him I would hire someone who was dependable, had a good track record, and was bursting with initiative— all the qualities George lacked or had lacked.

Growber agreed, and I knew George didn't have a chance. How could Growber trust a George he'd watched do the Times crossword and scribble lines of poetry for five years? And the rug? I knew the rug worried Growber. What would the other leaders think of a commander who hid his imperfections under cheap nylon fibers?

I had already consigned George's fate to fate, but I couldn't let it go. One last scheme fell into my lap. I was watching a fan drive smoke from the Cave a week before the big interview when I had the idea. George's rug did weird things in wind. Growber, because of a mild heart attack last year, was slowly becoming a health nut. Strong drafts and

George's rug. I saw a debacle. I saw George losing his composure before and after the interview. I saw Growber shaking his head no to George's application.

It wasn't a perfect plan; in fact, it was silly. But stopping George had become an idée fixe. I girded my loins and took Growber to lunch and casually mentioned a New York Times article on the beneficial effects of circulation, open windows, and drafts. Growber took the bait.

Since that lunch, the wind rose on the eighth floor. I bought paper weights. I wasn't sure what effect my ploy would have on George or his rug, but I soon found out. George's rug was smack in the path of Growber's jet stream. Soon his rug began playing little tricks with my eyes, dancing and cavorting on his head, almost as if it were animated.

Had I set him up?

"You certainly tried," said Barbara. "But who knows? Maybe Growber is worried his recommendation would hurt his own standing."

"I don't think that's an issue. The issue is George's replacement if he is promoted."

"It's a state job. From what you've told me, there are Georges and Dantes everywhere. Even if George makes it, you're probably going to get someone just like him."

"There are people as incompetent as George but who are sticklers for doing their time. And George has become a stickler anyway."

"Poor Dante. You've been fighting George as if it were Dante's Last Stand."

"I'm fighting for a way of life."

Barbara shook her head. "Which is humdrum, mediocre, and boring."

"It's not that boring."

It was going to be over soon. The weeks flew by, George worked industriously, and his rug rippled in the wind.

Then it was time for the big interview.

The wind was up. Miniature dust storms spun over the floor past the analysts' desks and over the cubicle partitions. I looked at George's rug. The first row of fibers held themselves stiffly in the air like troops advancing in a dubious battle.

Finally George disappeared in Growber's office and, as I'd hoped, Growber left the door open. I heard snatches of questions and answers. Then there was silence. The interview was lasting longer than it should. Then George appeared in the door, tie swept over his shoulder, wind ruffling his shirt, and his dome as shiny as a new penny. Where was the rug? Then I saw it; George was carrying it in his hand as a warrior might from a tough battle. I guessed George was making his pitch while Growber watched the rug; also that the rug lifted, did a pirouette on his head, and fell in George's lap.

The next day, George entered sans rug. It looked like I was going to work with Yul Brynner. A week later, George found they'd hired someone else for the Grade 23 slot. He was despondent, morose, beaten. But such is the resiliency of our species that a few days later, I saw the Times crossword on his desk and heard him quoting Frost in the bathroom. Growber growled, but even he was happy we were back to normal. Eventually Beryl left, and the roiled waters of George's pond have subsided, its sole inhabitant now happy and content.

Did I save us? Barbara had begged off, but I went to the Cave that night anyway. The night seemed empty. I worried about what I'd done in my favorite Greek diner, the Delta, then I worried it at home with Pollywog. I turned on the lamp over the dining room table and watched the fading light stream past the bars on the windows.

What about Dante Meno? I sensed something had changed. In acting to preserve the status quo, I'd seeded a cloud over my own inner landscape. Pollywog escaped my caresses. I brought out Conan Doyle. I scratched my head and watched two curly black hairs settle on the open page.

Offering

Chugga, chugga, chugga…clink.

Leona Stein lifted her beringed finger from her Ronson calculator. She lowered her eyes so they were eight inches under the art nouveau swirls of the stained-glass lamp which hung over the table. The sun shone brightly in the west, but it didn't illuminate much more than the bars on the window at the end of the studio. In the evening, most of the apartment was musty and dark, and the lamp light made a harsh oasis of the round oak table.

Michael Monroe sat in an armchair to the right of the fireplace, squinting at the pale light pouring through the bars in the window. For some time, those bars had seemed less real and more symbolic, bars that cut him off from the world, which, at that time, was Greenwich Village, New York, New York.

His gaze shifted from the bars to Leona then to the calculator. That sound meant something distasteful. And he felt drawn to find out, like a fluttering moth to a burning candle.

Michael sighed, heaved to his feet, and walked slowly over the brown pile carpet. He sat down opposite Leona. The light hurt his eyes.

Leona thrust her head under the lamp, making a shadow on the table. "Michael, we have to make more money."

Leona was a second-generation Russian Jew with dark curly hair and sloed eyes; Michael was a Midwestern WASP, tall, blond, blue-eyed. He made a fair counterpoint to Leona's dark hair and eyes, except now the light made her face a moon with a dark halo. They were polar opposites, destined to strike an uneasy balance over the round oak table with its cone of light, which stirred when the draft nudged the stained-glass lamp. Michael canted his head down a notch and made question marks of his fair eyebrows. "We will when you go back to work."

"You always ignore the real question."

What was the real question? He was sure of one thing: his real question wasn't Leona's real question. A year ago, he had been happily underemployed as a freelance editor. He read slim French Gallimard existentialist novels in Central Park. He contemplated Picasso's Goat in MOMA's sculpture garden. In the evenings, he hung around the edges of the literary scene in Greenwich Village, the Village, with its monuments to writers from Hawthorne and Poe to Kerouac. There was The Lion's Head with jackets of boozy authors stuck to the walls, the 55 Club with it drunken poets, the Blue Muse, the Village Gate. His own rejected short stories had moldered in the clichéd trunk, although someday, after he was famous, he'd bring them out, publish them. Everyone would see how brilliant he was, how nuanced.

In retrospect the increments, his increments, his slow trip to a Michael Monroe he sometimes didn't recognize, started in the Blue Muse. A drunken poet was quoting Whitman, when Leona sat down next to him. She plopped a huge burgundy bag on the bar, rummaged in the bag, retrieved a cigarette, and asked for a light. She was stunning with her tangled raven black hair, cheekbones, and sloed eyes. That night had a fantasy feel to it. She was charming, coy, alluring.

And she seemed charmed with his wit and looks. Before he could say "increment," they were in bed. Then a few months later, he moved out of his room and into Leona's apartment. A month after that, despite being able to get along on his editing jobs and her full-time accounting one, she conned him into a full-time job with Electronic Systems as a writer and trainer.

Everything was fine for months; then her back acted up and she went on sick leave. She went through her accrued vacation and now was on unpaid leave. In the last few months, when she wasn't depressed, she had become a hard-as-nails, entrenched, sarcastic opponent. Some nights he felt she was more attracted to strife than sex. She made up pseudo-issues and attacked them with a rising volley of words, like the tide slowly pulling down a sand castle.

But, finally, he was doing something. He'd been secretly looking in the "Furnished Apartments" section of the Times and had found an ad for an old hotel, the Rex, on the East Side. He'd called them and the desk clerk said they had a couple rooms and they would hold one for him for a deposit. It would work until he found a bigger place. Then he'd see about getting rid of that job.

Increments. He would control them.

Chugga, chugga, chugga..clink.

"The real question," Michael said, pugnaciously, "is you going back to work."

Leona smiled sarcastically and said, "Are you a doctor now?"

Michael rested his elbows on the table and his head on his hands. He stared directly into Leona's dark eyes. "He asks the same questions. How do you feel? Is it any better? You could say it's not better for the next fifteen years."

Leona brought her face closer. "I don't need your sarcasm, mister. Behind that blond-haired, blue-eyed fake Midwestern innocence is a very repressed person."

Michael squinted against the glare. "You've made yourself into a hermit. When it's sunny you close the drapes. On the weekends, you sleep all day and complain that you haven't done anything. You're barricading yourself against the world. Your back will never get better."

"I hate that job." He knew that, but it didn't make any difference. Leona had the ability of announcing her real motive and later returning to her bad back as if she'd never revealed a thing.

"Your back will stay bad as long as you want. What if I wasn't here?"

"Now you're leaving. When did this start?" Her eyebrows shot towards the tall ceiling. "Are you seeing someone else?"

He'd stumbled. Badly. He'd learned one thing about Leona over the last few months. He supposed she'd inherited it from her forbearers, who spun around in circles and threw salt over their shoulders: she was psychic. She could feel when he was evasive.

He had to strike back, and quickly. "When? I work twelve hours a day, shop, and cook because of your alleged bad back."

"There's something going on. I can feel it." Leona looked sorrowful, as if she knew he'd already decided to leave. Then her eyes went hard. "You always have a little word that has an edge on it. If it weren't for my back, you'd be looking for another place. You'd better sleep in the loft tonight."

That threat had become a mantra. "Fine. Maybe I'll get some sleep."

"Life can't be this boring," Leona pouted. "I need a vacation...or a break. Being out for a bad back isn't a vacation."

"As long as we have one income, we're not going past Fourteenth Street."

Leona sighed. "I have an appointment, Tuesday. If it's not too bad, I suppose I'll go back to that crummy job. But we still won't have any money. We're poor—we might as well face it: poor! poor! poor!" She looked distraught, be-ringed hand wound tight in her curly hair, soft eyebrows drooping over pained coal-black eyes. "We don't have enough money for lox and bagels at Sloan's. Everyone in the Village makes five times our income, and they're investing or buying a second house in the Catskills, or they're buying something—new TVs or DVD players—and we sit here like stone images staring at a dusty 17-inch Magnavox and an ancient VCR that went belly-up last night. It's embarrassing and boring, and it can't last."

Whenever she said "we," especially after telling him he had to sleep in the loft, he worried; he saw long stretches of time running past him and loping into a dim coupled future. And it hadn't been that bad until the VCR broke. Even when they'd reached an armed truce, they could always check out a flick. Last night, the VCR had chewed up My Little Chickadee, right after the opening credits. Yes. Lots of little things. Increments.

He wasn't sure how they got through the night. He had another beer, and Leona tried to read, but the busted VCR sat between them like a ghost. And when it was time to go to bed, he didn't sleep in the loft. And he didn't sleep well. He distrusted Leona when she compromised like that, when she said something, then took it back. Whenever she made a concession, the guilt rolled down the see-saw to his side.

That would change soon. At noon he'd withdraw the deposit for a room at the Rex. All he was leaving at Leona's were clothes and a couple books. After Leona cooled down—if she cooled down—he'd get them. He dressed, kissed a sleepy Leona, and ate a quick breakfast. Then he grabbed the black garbage bag and walked down the five flights to Tenth Street. He dropped the garbage in the can and started walking west towards Seventh to catch his bus. He felt better, much better than last night. The sun was shining, the crowds on Seventh animated, the traffic bustling. It was the start of a brand-new day.

He took the bus down to Canal Street, then walked the few blocks to Duane Square. Duane Square was close to the river, and between the buildings the Hudson sparkled. The distant scrum of New Jersey struggled through the smog.

He looked at the man feeding the pigeons in Duane Square, then the homeless man covered by a cardboard box at the other end. Michael sighed and pushed open the door of the ten-story building. A few minutes later, he sat at his desk staring at the loose pages of his presentation.

He spent the morning mixing text and the transparencies. In the afternoon, he'd do a dry run in one of the vacant training rooms. At moments when he was working, his dilemma with Leona troubled him. He'd think of the Rex, the deposit. Was he going to do it? He would help her with the rent until she went back to work. He had to admit, finally, he was ambivalent. If only their time together was easier and not strife-filled. Just before noon, he sighed and dialed the Rex to confirm he wanted the room. Increments worked both ways. Increments had trapped him with Leona, increments would get him out. He was taking the first tentative step.

He ate a quick lunch inside, then went to the cash machine on Canal Street and took out $100 for the deposit. Canal was a crowded mélange of shoppers, bargain hunters, electronic and second-hand stores wrapped in a haze of shish kebab smoke and grease. He hated worming his way through the loud lunch crowd, but that was what New York was about, especially if you had a job. He turned up Wooster to escape the crowd and found himself on a pleasantly deserted street. He still had fifteen minutes of his lunch break. Behind him, a mass of noise and smoke; ahead, a few rare minutes of solitude and peace.

"DVD player."

He looked to his left, then back towards Canal Street. A thin black man appeared through the haze of Canal. He approached him carrying a large box.

The black man slowed almost to a stop.

"New DVD player."

Then the man was off walking quickly towards the intersection of Wooster and Grand. The box he was carrying did look like a DVD box. It had cryptic lettering and a blue DVD player displayed on the cover.

Finally they were close to the end of the street, and the man stopped and looked back at him, and a weary smile broke over his face as he rested his box on a fire hydrant. He wiped his brow as if he were Sisyphus. "Boy that's heavy. You wouldn't want to buy a DVD player, would you?" He said it as if he hadn't already planted a subliminal message in his ear.

Michael glanced back towards Canal Street, as if he expected two policemen to emerge from the crowd. Past the black man, the intersection of Wooster was deserted. "I don't need a DVD player."

"I'm just trying to get rid of it, that's all. It's a nuisance carrying this thing around."

"Is it hot?" He knew that was bad taste, but it slipped out.

The guy smiled, put his finger to his lips and shook his head. "I can't say. All I know is that it's a Sharp DVD player with on-screen display, progressive scan..." The man peered at the box. "...MP3—whatever that is—slide show, remote control." The man shook his head as if he marveled that there was such a product.

"How much?" He half-doubted the man's story—Leona always said he was a sucker, that it was a wonder he'd survived until he met her.

"I was going to sell it for $300, but I have to get rid of it today. I'm having problems with the old lady."

He warmed to the man—he could appreciate old lady problems. "And—"

"Name's Henry. Yours?"

"Michael."

Henry put his hand on his chin. "How much? Tell you what. For you, $150. That's on-screen display, progressive scan—"

"I got it the first time." And he read it on the box. He began to have a weird feeling about that DVD player. Later, it was almost as he knew in that one moment what he was going to do and that it would turn out badly. It went beyond increments. It was a feeling of fate. He couldn't have turned and walked away. In a lightning second, he started thinking that player could be an offering, a leave-Michael-in-peace substitute for Leona's broken VCR. Leona couldn't say a word for a month. Sex, the easy evenings, would cycle back.

The Rex hotel or the DVD player? Player or Rex?

He knew he should step away. The black man smiling at him had just stolen a DVD from an electronics shop on Canal. He, Michael, could be arrested! So many reasons to turn and leave.

Before he could think rationally, he said, "I'd like to, man, but I don't have the money. I got a piddling-ass job and I can't afford an extra $150. Besides I don't know what I'm getting. You got to set these things up and see if they work."

"Does it look like I have a showroom? If I had a showroom, I'd charge you $300—but I don't. And I'm willing to bargain a little...not much, because I want to get my fair value out of it. This is capitalism—if you don't get out what you put into it, it's a losing proposition."

What had Henry put into it? Lifting it out of a showroom? "How do I know it works?"

"I don't know it works, either. But why wouldn't it? It was got right in the showroom."

"Could I see it?"

"Mikey, man, please. What if you don't want it? The next person I try to sell it to will see it's been opened and won't want it. You'll never find a better buy than this. I've always wanted a DVD player, but I can't afford it. I need the money for the rent and a little something for the old lady. But you look like you're ready for it. You're looking good. You got a good job. And won't that be a surprise for your wife!"

"Girlfriend."

"That won't last. Anyway, won't that be a big surprise?" Henry winked male complicity. Henry needed the money for his family; Michael needed the player to hold off Leona. They were both working men. Henry's work was just a little different.

"I only have $100. I won't have any more until Friday."

"I don't know, Mikey." He picked up the box, a frown creased his forehead. Then he elaborately put the box down. "You know, we're in this thing together. I know what it's like to never have enough money and to try to have a few nice things around. I'll sell it to you for $100."

Michael was tempted. But what if it didn't work? Leona would never let him forget that! "Could I think about it?"

"Michael, I like you, but this is a hot little item. I can't let my feelings get in the way of business. I could sell it to the next guy down Wooster for $150."

Michael felt tight in his stomach—he was doing something illegal, and he'd never dealt well with quandaries. Then he had a vision of Leona, speechless, in front of a shiny new DVD player. They would watch My Little Chickadee, make love, listen to jazz. Things would be like they were two months ago. He looked down Wooster, then towards Canal. No one was coming. He dug the money out of his pocket. He hesitated at the last minute. His hand trembled as he counted out five twenties into the man's open hand.

The man pocketed the money, sealed the exchange with a firm capitalist handshake, and handed him the DVD player. Then Henry walked briskly towards Canal Street, where he disappeared with a wave and a smile like a genie who had slipped in and out of a daydream. The weight of the box woke him up. It was heavy, but what was important was its spiritual weight. He had a peace offering, or a weapon in his battle with Leona. Sometimes they were the same.

At work, he hid the player under his desk and called Leona. He relished surprising her, but he needed a film to try out. They had to see something! He told her to get a DVD from Blockbuster.

She wanted the details, especially of the money he'd spent, but he had to work on his presentation. He left her in an aggravation of curiosity.

He tried concentrating on presenting the Inquiry Sub-system for the new Fiscal Upgraded System (FUS), but couldn't. He checked the DVD every fifteen minutes. It was always there—the blue image on the white manufacturer's box, the cryptic list of features, the remote control. It gave him an odd sense of finally being in a society he'd only seen from the outside.

On the way home, he hugged the box to his chest hoping it wouldn't get injured by the 1 IRT, which jerked to a stop more often than he remembered and whose riders aimed hard arms, legs, and elbows at his precious package. By the time he'd walked up to the fifth floor, his muscles ached.

A few minutes later, the box lay on the near side of the oak table, bathed in light. Leona wrapped her arm around him and they stared at the Sharp with on-screen control, progressive scan, MP3-ready, remote...

She stroked the box. "A DVD player, a real player. Wow!"

"Did you get a flick?"

Leona pointed to a jewel case on her desk, next to the calculator. "They're so much smaller than videos. You wonder how they can pack so much into such little space. I couldn't find My Little Chickadee at first, but they checked and someone had just turned it in. Hurry, hook it up."

Leona cracked the jewel case. "This is so thoughtful, Michael. So where did you buy it? How much did you pay? Let me read the guarantee."

"Later."

He felt a thrill as he started on the box. He slit the side with a knife, being careful not to damage the player.

When the top was off, he dug through the papers.

"Do they always put papers inside?" Leona was inquisitive—she was always like that—but when he explained things to her, she didn't listen.

"You have to protect the player. It's an expensive toy." He'd expected Styrofoam. He was sure they used Styrofoam or those foam peanuts. He had four or five crumpled papers on the floor when he saw the corner of the first brick. Later, he remembered it was crumbly and worn as if it had been taken from a wrecked building.

Bricks.

"What's that?!"

Michael flushed. He realized he hadn't done that since he'd fumbled his lines in the Merton High School production of Our Town. He was the paperboy. He only had two lines and forgot the second. But then there was more. He felt alone, completely isolated in a room that looked like a museum. He felt the enormous existential distance between himself and Leona. It was like Sartre's essay on Giacometti, comparing his diminishing figures to the huge spaces between people sitting next to each other in a post-war café.

"It appears to be a brick."

"What's it doing there?"

"I don't know." He carefully took out the other papers and uncovered three more bricks. Leona sat down after the second brick.

Bricks. Newspaper.

"Tell me it's a practical joke."

A thin black man—Henry?—with fake family problems had handed him The New York Times, a discarded Sharp DVD player box, and four medium-sized bricks. He'd protected those bricks on the subway as if they were fragile flowers. He'd hugged them to his chest.

"Does it take a special installation to hook these bricks up? Are you sure you can do it yourself? Let's see My Little Chickadee."

He stared at the mess on the floor. It was worse than Our Town. He'd taken his clothes off in front of a crowd. Increments. He'd engineered another fatal increment. Leona's sarcasm bit deep between his shoulders. "I, I—"

"Of course, the 'I' defense. Maybe you can cook them—a brick sauté. And how much did we pay?"

He heard his voice; it was thin and weak. "A hundred dollars."

Chugga, chugga, chugga...clink.

"Let's see; that makes twenty—no twenty-five—dollars a brick. Can you get some more?"

After an hour or so, Leona let up on him and tried to sooth his battered ego. But he had to get away from her.

Outside, he called the Rex and told them he wouldn't take the room at that time.

At that time. Really? Was the Rex still an option?

He soon walked numbly through the bustling streets of the Village. He stood outside the Blue Muse. He had gone into battle with the best of intentions, with resolve, and defeated himself. He hadn't controlled the increments.

Increments. Was it really about increments at all?

Maybe it was just about life, about one thing becoming another. We could look back and see increments, about what one could have done here or there. But wasn't that all hindsight? Well, control or not, he certainly didn't control the Leona situation...this time.

When he got back, Leona tried to coax him into bed, but he shook his head and stayed in the loft. He had penance to perform.

He stared at the beams in the loft and tried to ignore Leona's barely concealed eruptions of laughter. He wondered what Henry was doing. What was Henry seeing on his ceiling?

He could look for him tomorrow. What would he say? "Hey man—your bricks suck!" or "Hey man—they were bricks!" Nothing he could say wouldn't be obvious and make him look a bigger fool. On the other hand, you had to admire the guy's artistry. He'd taken discards, added greed, and sold him a dream. He was a real entrepreneur.

The beam was a foot from his nose, and a vision of the box floated in front of his eyes. It was a Sharp DVD player, on-screen programming, progressive scan, remote control—

Homecoming

A tall shape flitted back and forth in the full-length mirror in the closet. It finally stopped and the elements drew together. Audrey Lampton glanced at her reflection. She ignored the tall, slightly bent form, loose brown hair, jeans and white shirt, and went for the gray eyes. They were troubled. She tried to calm herself. She smiled as if sharing a joke with her image. But the smile quickly turned into a frown.

Audrey tensed. She felt the skin tighten over her face as her mouth pursed. She waited. The thin, keening sound was the wind in the trees in the back yard, only the wind.

Late last night, Robert, her ex-husband, called from Drake's Bar. He wanted to—had to—see her. She knew the Drake's Bar stages first hand. First he would be happy and loud, buy rounds, and flirt; then, afflicted by some slight, he would get moody. The punch line in the Robert-is-moody curve used to be Audrey. Not that he was physical. No, it was his stupidity which first started her thinking of divorce. No, she wasn't there for that last moronic Drake's Bar stage. Not for a long time.

She said no. He said he'd see her anyway.

She'd fretted about that all day. She gazed at timelines of projects on the computer monitor at Xpert Systems, but the dates, the people, the spring deadlines were meaningless, lines and boxes like mazes, where she was the rat. Driving home through the cold night, a few flakes fluttering down and disappearing on her windshield, her thoughts stayed in the car. Then she saw—or thought she saw—Robert's custom black Jaguar. It appeared between snow banks at the crest of a hill, then vanished.

Audrey turned away from her image. She quickly changed into gray sweats and white socks and strode into the living room with its sliding glass door, which peered like an eye over the back yard, its worn but comfortable gray sofa, the Panasonic TV, which she'd watched too often lately, and the solid oak table between the living room and kitchen. She paused in her trajectory and stared at the fireplace, stuck in the wall near the front.

A fire? Later.

Audrey opened the refrigerator. She tapped her long fingers on the door as if she were deciding what to make. The piercing refrigerator light drilled into her brain. She let the door swing slowly shut. She felt riveted to the kitchen floor. She felt alone, exposed. Again. It wasn't that she was afraid of Robert. Of course she was, she explained to herself. But it was more that she was afraid of what Robert stood for. Two dead years. He had taken her, won her, beguiled her away from what she was, an intelligent, competent manager of people, someone who thought and cared and made her into someone with history she didn't recognize.

During the time with Robert, she felt she was in a dream. But that dream had become dross, a heaviness around her heart. Depression. Prozac. History. She'd been transformed from an independent, happy, albeit manless, woman into a twentieth-century cliché.

Audrey made a G & T, went into the living room, sat on the sofa, and switched on the TV. She stared at her reflection in the sliding glass doors. It was winter. Outside, she barely made out the snow-covered yard. The indistinct branches of the oaks rimming her plot scratched the dark sky.

Audrey felt her heart sink as she stared at her image. She was bright, awkward, and had the slight hunch tall girls developed in school to get dates. Why did Robert like her? She supposed it was the attraction of opposites. She was bookish, absorbed, intense; Robert easy, off-handed. It wasn't love on either side. She thought once that he needed a smart wife as a kind of indirect compliment to himself, that because she was smart, he was too.

But that was too simplistic. She never guessed they'd marry. She sure never guessed they'd divorce either—after two years. She supposed the divorce was never far from her thoughts. It wasn't the details, the nasty details, the droning of the lawyers, the accusations. No, it wasn't the details. But she went over them anyway, trying to make them the issue.

Meeting in Drake's Bar. Robert was a cute, regular fella who was good with the ladies. The first night. Sex. Comfort. Then the marriage. Marriage was the death of love, again. Of course, she wasn't sure she—or Robert—was in love. It was just an exercise. Drake's Bar, baseball, droning announcers of TV sports. It was so maddeningly boring. It was over a year ago, when she told Robert she wanted a divorce, when she turned the first tiny gear in removing from her soul the canker Robert had become. Robert, curiously, wanted to hang on, as if she'd missed his signals that he was trying to tell her something. Then it got weird. First Robert's parents talked to her, then her own divorced parents—George and Sarah— cranked themselves down like separate deus ex machinas to the side of keeping up appearances. She told them in a funny way, which she wouldn't have done before she met Robert, that it was a training marriage, just like training wheels or a starter home.

It took Robert a long time to get the message. He thought that threatening her was a freebie which went along with being married to her once. The first time, right before the divorce, in a rage, more because it wasn't over, still wasn't over, she thought she'd give him a message, something, again, she wouldn't have done before she met him. She cut an old collection of his baseball hats into a thousand little pieces with an orange pair of self-sharpening scissors and mailed them to him. He left her a nastier message after that. She reciprocated by emptying all her drawers, throwing all of their photos in a pile, reducing them to thin glossy slivers, and mailing those to him.

Of course it wasn't over, but after he got those packets of garbage, the detritus of his marriage, he stopped. For a while. But just before the final papers, Robert started a new cat-and-mouse game with the phone. He called, beery and barely coherent, and threatened, usually from Drake's Bar.

There had been two post-divorce incidents. Once they had a shouting match in her driveway. She could almost see the fingers in the drapes and hear the whispers of her neighbors. The second was scarier. Robert had bulled his way inside her—formerly their—home. Fortunately Robert was too drunk to do anything. Afterwards, after the humiliation, she tried to make light of it. She imagined Robert was a reincarnated Toto, or whatever his name was from the Pink Panther flicks, lurking, waiting for her Clouzot on the toilet or in the bathtub. That time she'd called his father and told him to keep his moron on his leash, or she'd press charges and get a restraining order. It would be in all the papers. It would hurt his business.

Hurt business. That got John, the old man, whom she'd always sorta liked. Except when she started thinking about him, his own divorce, the way he boasted about his golf game and girlfriends, she thought: like father, like son.

The second incident, when she thought about it seriously and not as Pink Panther silliness, showed her that her marriage wasn't over and wouldn't be over until some defining event. She took a class in self-defense. She was unsure of her motives. She could always handle Robert intellectually. On the other hand, why play around with a self-described aggrieved man fueled with Bud Lite? It went against all her instincts, all she'd been brought up to believe in, the way she thought, the way she wanted to be in the world. But she did it.

The instructor was a mild-mannered ex-Green Beret who had a thing about women's self-defense and whom she thought took a shine to her, but it could have been that she had missed signals. Peter taught her and a group of twenty women—were they all there because of abusive men, or had they given into the reigning paranoia?—a few self-defense moves, but she finally got Peter's critical lesson: the best defense is a total absence of pity.

She hadn't had occasion to try that out on Robert or any other man. Maybe this was the time. He'd called last night; she thought she'd seen his Jag outside. Was it time?

She heard a key in the door. She jumped to her feet. Her drink hit the floor, staining the rug. The TV cast a thin flickering glow over the carpet, the growing stain. Out the window, the moon was peeking over the tops of the trees.

The light in the kitchen cast shadows over the silverware and dishes scattered on the counter.

The door opened slowly. She quit breathing, her hand knuckled across her mouth. She was almost relieved when she saw it was Robert.

He was wearing a windbreaker, which was open and showed a white shirt. He had a drunken grin on his face. The porch light threw his shadow almost to her feet. Total absence of pity. It was a hard thing for a woman to learn.

"I heard you had a new guy."

"Lots of them. There's Larry, Moe, and Curly, your buddies," she sneered. She knew better than to antagonize him, but all of a sudden, she was beyond diplomacy. She was trying to sort out her life, to build it moment by moment, day by day, but her broken marriage was right there in her cubicle at work, on her holidays, in her bedroom, demanding, keeping her off-balance.

"You haven't been too friendly lately, Aud."

"We've been divorced for a year. I don't get it; I really don't get it. You've got a passel of girlfriends. You've got your buddies. What could you possibly want with me?"

"Let's talk," he stammered. "I just want to talk."

"We talked for two years. Or, rather, I talked and you got drunk and stupid. It was a mistake. If you want to talk to somebody, let's talk to the police."

Robert moved closer. He was four feet away from her. She backed up.

"This is going to cost you, Robert. You don't know how much."

His face became contorted as if he'd held himself back

as long as he could. His head twitched and a tremor shook his body. "It'll be worth it, just to fuck you again."

Audrey could feel the twitch in her own face. She saw where she might stand, what she might do. She tried to remember the self-defense moves. Total absence of pity. "I guess you're right, Robert. Come here, baby."

Robert looked stunned for a brief second, then he grinned. She held out her arms. Robert stumbled forward and she quickly reached down, grabbed his ankle, and pulled up hard. Robert crashed on his back, but he rolled slowly to his right. He was an athlete once.

"Bitch."

It sounded like the last time. What she didn't understand—she supposed she'd never understand—was why. Robert was a cute guy. One of the reasons they broke up was that he had too many girlfriends. What did he have to prove? It stunned her that he kept putting his life, his job, everything on the line, just to get in a few hits on her.

Robert struggled to his feet, seemed to huddle on himself, and then lunged at her. She thought for a moment of surrendering, of letting him do whatever he wanted. He wouldn't kill her. She would be the aggrieved, battered woman. She would elicit sympathy from everyone. She would be pitied. She would sue.

She let him grab her. Then she grabbed his arm with her other hand, planted her foot, and spun him around. He crashed into the sofa and fell to the floor. Past him, the moon made ivory puddles on the deck. There was Robert's head, the moon, a few pieces of furniture which, despite the light, seemed foreign, the irritating glow from the TV. It was as if they were intrusions from a reality of solid things into their spiritual mano a mano.

Robert shrugged off what was probably dizziness and stood up, hitting his knee on the table. "Fuck me. Now, Aud. Now you're going to see."

He came at her again, his face contorted into a mask.

She backed up and Robert made a final, spastic lunge. She had backed up to the fireplace and her hand grazed a poker. It felt like slow motion, but she reached down, picked it up, and in a movement she wasn't sure she could make, hit Robert's knee.

"God," he yelled. "What are you doing!?"

When he reached for his knee, she tapped him on the head and watched him fall, slowly. He lay on the ground. He felt his head and then started crying. Then he gathered himself like a fetus and closed his eyes. She supposed she could kill him. He was helpless, out cold. She could cry self-defense. She shrugged and dropped the poker.

***

She wasn't sure what to do. She was sure he was all right except for his pride. She had the phone in her hand. She would call the police. They would pick Robert up. She would press charges which might or might not stick.

She dialed Robert's father.

After ten rings, he picked up. "Who the hell is this?"

She could imagine John's cute face, distorted and angry, and his thickening body. She almost cut the connection. "It's your ex-daughter-in-law, John."

"What do you want?" he said, worried.

She paused, waiting for the pause to sink in. "Robert's here."

"What the fuck is he doing there? Let me talk to him."

"He's not too compos mentis right now."

"What does that mean?" She detected his nervousness over the phone. She felt much better than she had a right to feel.

"It's kinda complicated, but I'll give you the big picture. Robert got drunk, somehow duped the key to the front door, barged in here, and assaulted me. But he was too drunk to do much harm."

"Let me talk to him!"

"No can do. He's out cold. We struggled and he hit his head. He's OK, but I thought I'd call you before I called the police."

"I'll be right over."

"Not so fast."

She could hear heavy breathing on the other end of the line. "I'm a little pissed off right now, and I want to tell you what I'm going to do." John didn't say a word, so she forged on. "First, I'm going to take a photo of Robert on the floor. Then I'm going to call the police. Then I'm going to call my lawyer and we're going to start a suit against Robert. Tomorrow, I'm going to send a letter recounting dates, threats and abuse, calls to the cops, etc., to your realty office, to the Sentinel, and I'm also going to take out an ad detailing Junior's stupidities. Am I going too fast?" She'd worked herself into a furor. She felt her heart banging in her chest and took a deep breath.

"There must be some way—"

"Just like divorce. I was the idiot, then. You and mojo here were going to take care of everything. That's why I got the house with a mortgage, and Bobo lives in one of the family properties and still drives his fucking Jaguar."

"Listen, we can work things out."

"I don't see how."

"I'll give you a check. Money."

"I know what a check is."

She glanced at Robert, then thought of all the abuse she'd taken during their marriage and in the last year. The late night calls. What got her while she thought about it was that he still thought he was impervious to prosecution, to jail. On the other hand, if she took the old man's money, the old man would make sure Robert behaved. And she'd have the money. It had a vague blackmail air to it, but with enough money she could leave, take a trip, get away.

John said, "How much?"

"A hundred grand, the price of his Jaguar."

"It's blackmail."

"Fuck you, John. You mentioned it, not me."

"I'll bring a check."

"You do that. And if there's any reneging, I'll do everything I said and more."

There was a pause as if John were thinking that over. Then he hung up. It looked like it was a go. Audrey checked Robert. He was breathing. The moon was still shining on the balcony. There was a vampire-type Outer Limits on the tube—weren't they all blood and gore and just-risen-from-the-grave stories?—which offered an odd counterpoint to Robert, who seemed wound around some cold center of hatred like a pretzel.

She made herself a drink, picked up one of the chairs from the kitchen, and sat near the door with it cracked open. John drove up five minutes later. He looked left and right, as if he were seeing if the neighbors were up, then he walked swiftly up the walk and stood before her. He wore a light jacket and boots, but one shoelace wasn't tied.

"Check, please."

John handed her the check, but he was looking over her shoulder.

It was made out properly to her for a hundred thousand dollars. She moved to the side and said, "He's all yours."

Robert wasn't moving. On an impulse, she went to the kitchen and ran some cold water in a glass and then over a towel. She came back and gave John the towel and set the glass of water down on the table.

"Bobbie," said John. He held the towel to his face and rubbed it slightly. Robert blinked then opened his eyes. "I suppose I should take him to a hospital."

"But you won't," said Audrey. "You'd have to tell them why. He's got a head of granite. Take him tomorrow."

"You know," said John, ruefully, "I always liked you, but I could never see how you two got together. You're talented, smart as a whip. Bobbie never really cared about proving himself, but he's a good salesman."

"He is your problem and not your problem, John. After a while people have to live with their own blunders."

"Where am I?" said Robert.

"You're coming with me for a while," said John.

"Where's the bitch?"

"No bitches here, Bobbie, just Audrey."

Robert looked at her, then lapsed into a stunned silence.

John helped him up and they stumbled towards the door. "The check will be good tomorrow." John said.

"I guessed it would be," said Audrey.

"Come on, cowboy."

John helped Robert to the door, then the two of them made slow progress to John's Suburban. Audrey paused, then strode past them and opened the side door. A few seconds later, Robert curled up on the seat.

John started the car, and she watched him turn around the circle and leave. His lights blinked at the stop sign, then turned and disappeared.

Audrey walked slowly up the sidewalk. When she got inside, she locked the door, then collapsed on a chair as if she'd been holding her breath. The moon made light on the balcony and touched John's check. It seemed curiously curled and vulnerable. What did it mean? It meant a lot of things. Freedom. But at the same time, it meant failure. It was like the final seal on her marriage, on the mistake. She picked up the check and waved it back and forth as if to see if it was real.

She thought of tearing it into shreds like she'd done with Robert's baseball caps and photos, but then she thought, no. That would be a grand gesture, another nail in the coffin of the past...but wasn't the future what she needed? Travel, a new job, a new perspective.

Hoot, hoot, hoot.

She tried to penetrate the moon glow. There was an owl out there beyond the balcony, beyond the back yard, in a small patch of pine two hundred yards away. The Nosferatu of the bird world. She'd looked for it a score of times, but it remained elusive. She decided to give up finding it; some things should remain a mystery.

JUST DESSERTS

Double Chocolate Fudge Cheesecake, Double-Baked Chocolate-Almond Croissants.

Double, double, double!

Dessert Plus was the most popular pastry shop in the Castro/Market/Duboce Triangle in San Francisco. It was an old narrow brick building with piles of carrot cakes, thick juicy pies, chocolate-topped macaroons, cheesecakes, and chocolate éclairs in two large glass-enclosed display cases in front and a smaller display of sticky buns, blueberry scones, morning buns, and croissants near the checkout counter in the middle of the store. Across from the pastries and desserts were small tables crammed into the narrow space, and at the end of the store were steps leading up to an expansive tree-lined patio.

Three people had just collected their coffees and pastries from the checkout counter. Chriss Mock smiled ritually at the counter person—who was red-haired and sported three earrings and an opal nose stud—and started towards the patio; David Burgess smirked and followed Chriss, and Linda Vasquez held back, smiled, thanked the woman for her defat latte, deposited a dollar in the tip jar, and walked slowly after Chriss and David. That day, the three were the best dressed in Dessert Plus. Chriss was the older man, around forty, and wore a loosened tie and a barely wrinkled $500 Armani suit, a flashy gold watch, and a diamond-encrusted wedding ring. David wore a crisp black suit and light blue tie, and Linda wore a simple dark blue business suit that accentuated her curves and a variety of rings on each hand minus a wedding ring.

They moved slowly, balancing their drinks and pastries like a squad of scouts from the business world through a casual older and hip mostly gay morning crowd. They glanced at the varnished tables—and serious people typing on laptops or reading papers or talking to neighbors at the small tables— and stepped carefully out the open glass door and through the spread of ferns palming three aged concrete steps to the patio. In the patio, they regarded the patio denizens, smiled a last official smile, and casually appropriated a large table.

The patio was full of a few large metal tables and chairs and many smaller ones, which that day were mostly taken with a younger crowd reading or talking or working on Mac-Books. The patio was cool, and clumps of heart-shaped leaves from the surrounding Lombardy poplars lay on the concrete. The patio had the air of a secluded oasis from the city and the thrum of traffic on Market and Church.

Chriss was a junior VP at Tower. He was an athletic-looking tall man with pale hair, a pinched fair face, and light wire-rim glasses which slid down a narrow sunburned nose. At home, in a three-bedroom house in Walnut Creek, he had a wife, Megan, who was cute, once, and who was now vulnerable and loud. He also had a small daughter and a son on the way.

What a crock, he thought: evaluating provisional agents. David was too stocky, too soft, and too uninteresting. He was surprised he'd made any sales with his short straight brown hair, brown eyes, and a reddish-hued piggish face. Linda Latina was different. He had to hide his—what should he call it?—lust. He'd seen her at the Tower and had the groin-grinding feelings he had with most attractive women, but this close her coffee-colored, slightly heavy body with its soft black eyebrows, full lips, light pink lipstick, and slight décolletage, his randiness peaked. Her lips around his cock. Her legs sprawling in the air. Tits flopping askew. A little anal action.

Time to be careful. He'd already given her a too-long look. But had she reciprocated? Was there a hint of liaison, of danger, in those dark brow-shaded eyes?

The agents sat across from Chriss, smiled, looked serious, and complimented him on his choice of Dessert Plus, although they had exchanged glances while they arranged their coffee and confections.

Chriss: "Guessing why I chose this place?"

Linda: "I sometimes come here for coffee." She paused, frowned, smiled. "But not for an evaluation. I like it."

Chriss smiled back.

David: "It's unconventional and kinda cool."

Chriss: "It's disorienting like selling. You have to think on your feet."

Chriss just threw that out. He wasn't sure why he used Dessert Plus. Once, he'd explained to his wife that it was like having his finger on the direction of America, but that was too simple and possibly wrong. He'd learned it was a window into a world alien to the one he chose to inhabit, a sleepy culture where the driving force was a naive, exaggerated—but poor—openness. As for the evaluation, he was trying to make it as painless as he could. The Latina was the only thing that made it barely tolerable.

Chriss pushed his glasses back to the bridge of his nose

and tapped a silver pen inscribed "The Tower" on a notebook he'd taken from his briefcase and opened. Chriss practiced what he called the "open" interview, which meant, roughly, that he passed people he liked and failed those he didn't on the supposition that if he liked them, so would the customers. He had forms and boxes for sales, projected sales, personality, and overall performance, and usually he pretended to write in them but doodled instead, making diamonds or squares, figures he filled in with light hashing. The boxes were unimportant, and he sometimes pulled scores out of the air the way he used to conjure sins for St. Mary's dark confessionals. He was sure the priests did the same, feeling the air for a phony penance to match a phony sin. Jordan—slightly older, slightly more senior—had advised him to use the forms, but he'd thanked him and continued with his hunches when he had to do evaluations at all.

He'd glanced at David's progress sheet and seen he'd sold three units, which was light for a year. Linda had only been an agent for six months according to Conroy, and he didn't have time to look at her progress sheet. If she sold anything, she'd tell him.

"Let's start with David." Chriss leaned back as David leaned forward. Linda put down her latte and held herself slightly away from David and the table as if she were going to judge David too.

Chriss glanced at Linda, his gaze lingering over her décolletage, but he quickly turned to David when Linda looked up.

"I'd like to talk units," said David. "I've sold six this year, and I've got two more in the pipeline that will bring it up to eight. Eight is a good year. I'm successful because I think on my feet and have a sixth sense about customers; you can't waste time in this business. You have to strike fast, regardless of who or what you like." David lowered his voice and Linda leaned forward to hear him. "Take the people here, for example; it would be easy to get rid of most of them. Initial impressions are rarely wrong. Go for it! Do it!"

Six units and two more on the way? Where was that on David's progress report? Had he missed it? Of course, David had repeated what he'd said about thinking on his feet and announced the golden rule: the bottom-line. What mattered was the bank and the money. And you couldn't waste time getting there.

David threw in a few more anecdotes about the shape of the units he'd sold and his aggressive personality, but Chriss had already made his initial estimate and drew pointy carets around one of the boxes. Just as David finished and leaned back in his chair, there was a thud near the glass doors to the patio, and the three agents turned to see a heavy young man panting on his back with what looked like strawberry cheesecake on his lips. He lay like a beached sea lion for a few seconds, blocking the path to the patio, before two be-ringed women warned everyone to stand back, jumped down the stairs, and began pumping on his chest in their version of the Heimlich.

A frown edged Chriss' usual half-smile. "That should teach us about greed. Greed is good for everybody; it's what drives America, the virtue of selfishness. But—" Chriss paused, and David and Linda turned away from the incident and back to Chriss. "But you can choke on too much." A siren grew louder, and soon two EM personnel hustled into Dessert Plus and worked over the young man. Finally, more

EMs crowded into the small space, clicked out a gurney, and threaded their way through the narrow path to the street.

Chriss listened to the conversational buzz from the surrounding tables, mused for a few moments about whether his Chriss-ism was appropriate, but he quickly directed his thoughts back to the interview. The Tower was at the bottom of a business cycle, and he guessed either David or Linda had to go; there had even been talk of trimming one of the VPs. Chriss knew it was Jordan. Jordan was old and old-fashioned, and he had to make way for new blood, new ideas, new energy. The business world had a Darwinian elegance that Chriss appreciated. He knew he was on Conroy's short list for senior VP: it was a cycle, an inevitable occurrence, a hymn to the fittest.

A leaf landed on the table and Chriss brushed it off. "Linda, take a crack at it?" And, thought Chriss, it better be good. His sexual fantasies about Linda aside, she had to produce. He had initially given her points for choosing a non-fat latte. David had, typically, gorged himself on a double-mocha latte and marbled cheesecake. But David had come back with his primitive and aggressive bottom-line disregard for the late morning non-working mostly gay crowd in Dessert Plus and had taken the lead.

Chriss mused about where and how he could ravage Linda, while she fussed with her slim burgundy valise, closed it, squared it to the table, and formed her arms into a triangle above it. She seemed oddly poised for a provisional agent.

Linda: "I could talk about units, but what's important is the future. Take Dessert Plus. Many agents would try to get rid of someone with a ring in their nose and blue streaks in their hair, but you know something?" Linda paused for suspense the way Chriss had. Chriss frowned. Linda edged slightly forward. "It's obvious some of them have money. They hang out here and go to bars and eat where they want. They likely never thought of working. Either they're trust-fund babies or their parents have money, which is even better." Linda concluded with a few things about how restructuring deals could make the Tower's offerings more attractive.

David leaned back in his chair with a mocking smile. No units?

Chriss frowned. If so, she was history. Too bad. If she'd stayed he could have arranged a dinner and possibly a liaison. He could see it in her eyes, the slight invitation, the way she moistened her pink lipstick with the tip of her tongue, the way she watched him sit, handle himself, his commanding voice.

Chriss brushed away a leaf floating down from a poplar and knocked over his latte. He quickly picked up his glass, but the brown liquid and light foam spread and soaked the bottom of the briefcase he'd casually thrown on the table.

"Shit. Excuse my French, Linda."

Linda and David watched the brown liquid, and Chriss put his evaluation pad on the empty seat. He wiped off his briefcase with a napkin and dabbed at the light brown puddle, but it quickly soaked the napkin, and he left it in the middle of the puddle, waving in an afternoon breeze. Chriss grimaced at it, excused himself, and went off in search of a Dessert Plus worker.

"What do you think of him?" Linda said.

David reached over the table, retrieved the evaluation form from the chair, and flipped it over. He smiled when he saw the scribbles and turned the form so Linda could read it. David put the form back then said, "I heard he did that. He's a dickhead. He may have been a good agent once, not now."

"I've heard that. How did you know?"

"Gossip. Jordan. Chriss has delusions...maybe everyone does who's been around for a while. They all think they're gods. But they're not: they don't produce, they don't stay. You think they'd keep Chriss around to do evaluations?"

Linda smiled. "No."

"Say, how many have you sold?"

Linda mused, "One, but it hasn't been registered yet."

David grimaced then said consolingly, "At least it's something. Still, that's not many."

Linda seemed to think about what David said. Finally she said, "It was a difficult sale."

David waved his hand dismissively. "You've only been on board six months; you'll sell more. Listen, we're both going to stay; he's the one on the way out. Even if you hadn't sold a unit and he gave you a lousy recommendation, you'd stay. You're young and sharp looking. You'll score. All he did last year was talk and act like a VP."

Linda shook her head, laughed. "Was that a come on?"

David, smiling devilishly, "Nah, I'm gay. Not my sex."

"I thought so. But thanks for the compliment."

"What about him? He's been drooling over you."

"Funny, isn't it? He stares at me, fantasizes, then scurries back into his upright act. I wonder if he's that transparent with clients." Linda watched David's expression, then made up her mind about something. "I still think new markets are the answer: unconventional markets, unconventional financing."

"I sold six units, soon eight. Find those people—that's your answer."

Linda smiled, seeming to agree with David. "Okay."

***

Chriss talked to a worker (white, female, rings, wallet, frozen ragamuffin smile) and told her where the mess was. He glanced towards the patio and seemed to make up his mind. He checked that the bathroom was unoccupied and went in, locked the door, and took out his cell.

Chriss asked Sabrina, another VP, about Linda.

"I think she worked with Conroy on the King account."

" What? She's a provisional agent!"

"I don't know much about her. I could be wrong."

A crystal of doubt quickly lodged itself in Chriss' confidence. Chriss had sold three units when he'd started five years ago. He was the consummate salesman, polished, smooth, although he hadn't done that well in a long time—no one had. He'd been surprised David had done so well and decided to check his figures when he got back to the office. As for Linda Latina, she had become an enigma.

Chriss smiled broadly as he sat down. The table was cleaned up, and the two agents looked at him expectantly. An anorexic woman and crossword puzzle-solver whom Chriss had seen before looked at him, rubbed the puzzle one more time, frowned, got up, and slowly walked out under the ferns. A tall black man watched the anorexic woman leave, sighed, opened his notebook, watched Chriss for a few beats, then busied himself in his open notebook.

Chriss tapped his pen on the table, making a soft staccato beat. He glanced at Linda. He felt a slight change in the atmosphere. Had Linda's expression changed? She seemed bored. He glanced at David. Was that a smirk?

"So, Linda. I assume you haven't sold anything. Any prospects?"

Linda sat back in her chair and regarded Chriss as if she were wondering what to say. "I have sold one, but it hasn't been registered yet."

"That's not a lot."

"It was a hard sale."

Chriss waved of his hand. "All sales are hard. Of course, if it was big."

"I think it was."

Chriss glanced quickly at David, who looked up from his own doodling. "They don't let provisional agents work on big sales."

"I suppose that's true. I was working late one night, and so was Conroy. We started talking and I mentioned how I would structure some deals differently. He seemed to like it."

Chriss felt sick. What had they done to him? He tried to remember what Conroy had said. Had he smiled? Did he want to pit these young agents against him? It was bad, worse. David had sold more units and the coy Linda...

The interview was slipping away from him, that is, if he ever had control of it. Chriss shook his head slightly. No. It was his imagination. He was in charge. As for the evaluations, David was a greedy slob, but he was traditional and could be counted on to behave. Linda's reluctance to tell him what she'd sold and to whom made him think she was playing with him. Another provisional agent who hadn't produced would have been fired. Unconventional markets, new structures. What a crock. Maybe she and Conroy had a fling? The old goat wasn't above it.

A homeless man who escaped the vigilance of the Dessert Plus workers limped through the opening to the patio. He sized up the people and brought out a small note card. He made the rounds slowly. Surreptitiously, he consumed a half-eaten croissant. He snagged a couple dollars from a mixed-age lesbian couple laughing about feminism and liberated sex. He collected another dollar from a long-bearded man who sat near the crumpled paper of the anorexic puzzle-solver.

He approached evaluator and evaluatees.

David waved him away.

The man smiled and held out his card towards Linda. Bits of croissant flecked the sleeves of his coat. He explained through his gestures his hopelessness. His face, contrite, bent further and came up, eyebrows pointed with a fractal of hope.

Linda clicked open her purse, took out two dollars, and placed them in the smudged hand of the homeless man. The homeless man bowed and thanked her with his eyes.

Chriss and David shook their heads, almost in unison.

Linda looked up and said, seriously, "He's certainly not a client, but you have to see him as a fellow human being. People sense that. And to get back to my first point, there are some people here that are potential clients."

Chriss stepped in, his wire-rims slipping further down his nose. "Linda, we got your drift. The point is that in some cases, you don't have to do somersaults to evaluate potential clients."

At this point, the object of their discussion thrust his card under Chriss' wire-rim glasses. Chriss looked at it, wondered about the strange contours of the evaluation, smiled weakly, produced a quarter, and put it in the man's hand. The man looked at the quarter, placed it firmly on the table in front of Chriss, bowed grandly, turned, and left.

Chriss smirked, shook his head, and raised his latte to take a final sip, but lowered it when he saw it was empty.

VERSIONS

Karl Megan—forty-five, his youthful huskiness turned towards thickness, his hair wavy but silvered—walked over Russian Hill in San Francisco, as he had for most of ten years, and down the steep slope of Union Street. At the liquor store on the corner of Union and Columbus, he noticed the Chinese seniors dotting the green patch of Washington Square Park across the intersection. A hundred seniors swayed, bent, and followed, or tried to follow, the Tai Chi forms. It was a curiosity, a North Beach oddity Karl would trot out at cocktail parties when he'd had a few drinks. For the first time, Karl walked across Columbus and joined them. He watched the leader at the corner near the church. Karl lifted his leg, held it, thrust his arms out slowly, and tried to feel what they felt. His mind felt empty; his leg felt like a log. He wobbled and dropped his leg. The thin, wrinkled men and women around him had their legs up. He felt clumsy and heavy, a too-white, too-tall intruder.

Karl shrugged, smiled to a wizened woman who didn't smile back, then turned and strode off purposefully towards upper Grant Avenue and the PC Perfect office. Karl had opened the office every morning for ten years, and he was still the first one, even though he'd sold PC Perfect to Bobby Lee Harmon of Dallas, Texas. The sale was a great moment and a sad one—bittersweet was the word, Karl told Darla, his wife. It completed a dream, a quest. He and Darla were secure, finally. He should have forged on to the next stage of his life, whatever that was. But Bobby Lee asked him to stay on for a few months to help with the transition and to work on the next version of PC Perfect. Karl said yes—he'd been handed a reprieve. His routines were intact, the core PC Perfect staff intact, and he was designing the new version. A reprieve, yes, but he felt as if he were pretending to be himself.

Karl unlocked the door then walked quickly to the alarm behind the receptionist's desk. His thick forefinger punched in his code. Seeing the LCD read-out made Karl remember, again, that he had to delete the codes of those employees—David, Leo, Sandra, and Mark—who had been laid off. Could a person be redundant? Sandra and Mark were new, but David and Leo were long-term programmers, older and higher paid than the two younger programmers who were kept. It was a real crisis in their lives. He tried to joke with them while they stuffed their plants, books, CDs, and Dilbert strips into large brown grocery bags. But it was awful, one of the worst moments of his life. He felt clumsy, ham-handed, his concern hollow.

Karl flipped the light switch and lights blazed on the ground floor, lighting up the reception, Mary Robbins' cluttered desk in the middle of the large airy space, Sales at the far end. Karl climbed the stairs to the mezzanine, walked past Bobby Lee's temporary office, and stepped into his office. His office was open on the mezzanine side, and the three walls were lined with photos, the desks stacked with trade journals, an excellence award, a vase which hadn't held a flower for a month. Karl sat down in front of his PC, but he looked up at a dimly lit photo of a company outing to the Russian River. Everyone was waving. Ed Barnes, his head of engineering, was there, as usual. Mary was there, as were the two redundant programmers. A tide of regret washed over Karl. Purpose, the clichéd company-as-family, was something he had believed in. His company, his employees' company. He gave bonuses, he worried about each of them, he gave them time off for everything. It was his life. All over. PC Perfect had become a commodity, a token in a big game with abstract, impersonal rules.

Karl shook his head as if to get rid of a pesky fly and got down to work. He fired up his PC and had started working on his presentation for the technical meeting that afternoon, when he heard the "mornings" and "hellos" of his staff. He turned to do his morning rounds of greetings, when he saw Bobby Lee disappear into his temporary office.

Karl frowned, then got up and walked over to Bobby Lee's office. "Got a minute?" Karl said. Karl didn't like Bobby Lee, the rail-thin, black-eyed Texan who bought PC Perfect. When they signed the papers, Bobby Lee had his Dobermans in administration, sales, and distribution in minutes. It reminded Karl of Napoleon's takeover in Animal Farm. When the dust settled, his programming staff had been cut in two, his office manager, Sandra, fired, and the marketing part of Sales and Marketing sent to Dallas. Karl had watched the whole unravel helplessly; of course, he had his money and the appearance of his old role, but it was a spiritual disaster.

Bobby Lee gave him a quick smile, then it dissolved in the bunched circles around his thin mouth. "Sit down," said Bobby Lee. He bent over a spreadsheet, which took up half of his desk, and circled two rows of figures. He peered at what he'd circled, then looked up at Karl.

Karl sat down next to Bobby Lee's Dallas Cowboys

pencil holder, and Bobby Lee flicked an imaginary piece of dust off his spreadsheet, leaned back in his chair, and made a long teepee of his hands, as if the teepee were a vortex for focusing his attention. "Ready for the technical meeting?" Karl said, getting to the point.

"Technical meeting? Wait a darn minute." Bobby Lee pulled his laptop on top of his spreadsheet and clicked on his planner. The planner bloomed on the screen and Bobby Lee scanned his appointments. "That's right; ah plumb forgot. Must be age. Let's see, I'm due at the airport at five. Hmm."

Bobby Lee always seemed to have his head in a spreadsheet, and he had a sickening "old boy" manner that made Karl distrust him on instinct. They'd eaten lunch three times a week for a month, and they still talked past each other. Of course, Bobby Lee had a family, two small girls, and a dog named Bat. "The meeting about the next version of PC Perfect."

"Course," Bobby Lee said. "Know all about it."

"This version has features our customers requested," Karl said, finessing Bobby Lee's obvious disinterest. "It solves translation problems and fixes outstanding bugs."

Bobby Lee threw his pen on the table and leaned back in his chair. "You've got a mighty fine product right now. I wouldn't have bought your company otherwise."

"A month for testing and QA. It would be faster with those programmers you fired."

Bobby Lee smiled, then rocked forward. "They had to go, Karl—no room on the spreadsheet. And this new version, you tell us about it in the meeting. I want to see what my boys have to say about it."

"I thought you'd want to get a heads-up." Karl got up brusquely. "I can wait."

Bobby Lee winked at him. "Plenty of time, Karl. Plenty of time."

Karl paused at the top of the stairs and ran his hand through his hair. He felt as if he'd been in the first skirmish of the day, except he didn't understand exactly why. Karl heard Don and the rest of the sales force cracking jokes in the far reaches of the main floor. Mary Robbins looked up from her desk and yelled good morning. Karl waved to Mary, then he popped his head into the shared cubicle of Dan and Mike, his remaining programmers, to say hello. Then he went to see Ed Barnes. He was making his morning rounds as usual. It felt right and false at the same time. When the new version came out, his team would hand it over to someone else. He wondered if there would be a celebration and another framed photo on the wall. Somehow he doubted it.

***

Karl and Ed Barnes went to lunch as usual. He and Ed—all three hundred and fifty pounds of him with his pink bald head and his cascading double chins—had fought a lot of technical battles in the last six years.

They ate at Café Puccini on Columbus, a short walk from the PC Perfect offices. Through the plate-glass windows, Karl saw tourists crowding up as they made their way through the flimsy green metal tables and chairs on the sidewalk in front of the café. Beyond the foot traffic, cars headed towards the Transamerica Building or the wharf. Karl watched a red

Mustang circling Washington Square Park looking vainly for a parking place.

An aria wafted through the café. Karl speared the lettuce in his antipasto; Ed picked up an eggplant parmesan hero with his soft sausage fingers and stuffed a quarter of it into his mouth. Sauce dripped on the table and spotted Ed's shirt. Karl watched Ed. It was a problem of lightness, heaviness. Light was Tai Chi, heavy an unspecified problem, small penis, large mouth, a disjuncture. Karl knew he was overweight, thick, but Ed always made him feel thin.

"I'm going to miss programming," Karl said. "But Darla's right: lining up bits and bytes? There's opera, bridge club, travel, Hawaii next month, Australia after that. I don't know how I had time for a company."

"I'll never give up programming," said Ed. "There is the challenge, seeing everything work. You don't need other people for that."

Karl smiled, filled with a thought that had the past in it. He thought of the first version of PC Perfect, the one he'd coded on his own. He'd felt like Ed during that time. "Are you ready for this meeting? Bobby Lee and his 'boys'— does he really talk like that? It sounds like he's rounding up a posse."

Ed swallowed and said, "His 'boys' will do what he wants or what they think he wants."

"They have wet dreams of spreadsheets," Karl said.

Ed paused, then looked at Karl expectantly. "What do you think they want?"

Karl put his fork down. "What does that mean? We've talked this out ad infinitum."

Ed wiped his lips on a napkin and threw it on the table. "It's a feeling."

"Tell me." Karl ran his thick fingers through his salt-and-pepper hair, a gesture Darla said he made when he was angry. He saw a solitary figure in the distance performing—was performing the right word?—Tai Chi forms in the park. The man was young, slim with thin corded muscles, and expert. How long it would take him to learn, to get past bumbling? Now what was Ed worried about?

Ed shook his head, then picked up the last bit of the eggplant and stuffed it in his mouth. "Don says Bobby Lee is splitting the product into pieces," Ed said. "Jacking up maintenance and selling it through Harmon Software. Don thinks that Sales will go to Texas."

"Bobby Lee told me he was going to keep the rest of the company here," said Karl.

"He's not interested in development," Ed said.

Karl picked up his fork and tapped it on his plate, not interested in eating. Ed had tapped into his own misgivings, a gut feeling he had about Bobby Lee, about what the "transition" was all about. "Bottom line, bottom line, that's what it's all about. He wanted me to stay on to help with this new version."

"I think he wanted you to stay to keep the rest of us here."

Karl thought about how Mary, Ed, and Don had stayed on despite disliking Bobby Lee and his gang. "I've thought about that, but I still think he wants this new version. Why not? Maybe he's waiting to develop it his own way," Karl said.

"If he doesn't do it now, he's not going to do it later. I

could be wrong, no doubt of it. Karl," Ed said, almost tenderly, "you built a nice little company. We've had a lot of good times. Why stay around? It's masochistic."

Karl watched the traffic. "I did it for the rest of you and the product, I suppose."

Ed shook his head. "It would be nice to tie up the loose ends with this version."

"We will," Karl said, although, for the first time, he wasn't sure.

***

At PC Perfect, Karl talked to Mary Robbins about what she was going to say in the technical meeting. Then he talked to Don Farina, head of Sales and Marketing. He hadn't talked to Don as much as he would have liked to since Bobby Lee took over. Don was a short, stocky Sicilian with thinning hair and a booming voice who could sell anything. Don looked up at his knock, and a look of surprise surfaced then receded into Don's salesman smile.

Karl sifted his thoughts. "Are you ready for this meeting?" Karl said.

Don glanced at his planner, then came back to Karl. "The new version?"

"Our last hurrah," Karl said.

Don took off his thick black-framed glasses, placed them on his desk, and rubbed his eyes. Then he said, "I'm ready; I don't know if Bobby Lee is."

"Why are these reservations surfacing today?"

"We've talked about what they're going to do with the

company, but then we got caught up with just trying to keep up. I tried to talk to you a couple of times last week," Don said. "You were too busy."

Karl clasped his fleshy, strong hands together. "Tell me."

"Bobby Lee is splitting the product. We can make money selling the current features."

"We need new features. We always need new features."

"I'm not disagreeing, but I'm not the one you have to convince."

"Convince?" Karl said, irritated. "I never thought I'd have to convince anyone."

Karl got up and went back to his office. "Convince?" Had he been duped? Was his reprieve a smokescreen, a too-simple plan for keeping everyone happy until there were more changes? He saw Bobby Lee was in a conference with two of his "boys." What if there wasn't a new version of PC Perfect? Was that the message under the false routine of the past month?

✳✳✳

The technical meeting. Bobby Lee and his "boys" lined up on one side of the long conference table and Karl's side lined up on the other—as if they were going to have a real gunfight. Karl disliked Bobby's boys by instinct—they were clean-cut, newly minted MBAs with suits and ties. They'd cut his staff. They'd fired his programmers. They knew diddly about programming. They did know how to talk Bobby Lee's bottom-line jargon. Vertical integration, horizontal integration. Screw the direction; you still had to sell a product.

Karl's side was the usual jeans, T-shirts, and sweatshirts.

Karl flipped off the light and gave his presentation. He showed the bug fixes and the features of the new version. After an hour, he flipped the light back on, and Ed talked earnestly about the short development time and its low cost. Then Don gave his usual excited pep-talk about market share and sales figures. Mary gave anecdotes about what their two hundred customers wanted.

Old days, old successes. He felt proud of the company he'd sold.

When Bobby Lee asked his "boys" about funding the project—the punch line—Karl's attention wandered to the framed photos on the wall of the conference room. There was PC Perfect's last outing on a Hornblower yacht, a tour of the bay, Ed in back, an enormous white shirt billowing in the wind like the sails. Mary, Don, the rest of the staff were holding the rail and waving. The sentiment, or sentimentality, hit Karl again. There had been so many meetings, so many projects, so many versions. Was this really the last version?

When he came back to those real faces at the meeting, he heard Bobby Lee's perky MBAs saying there was no money for a new version. Then they outlined their plan—the plan they'd been working on for a month—for merging PC Perfect into Harmon Software.

Karl shook himself out of his reverie. "Wait," he said, pointing his thick finger at Bobby Lee's "boys." "You know flat-out shit about software development. Why are you—"

"Hey Karl," Bobby Lee said, getting half out of his chair and leaning across the table, "let's keep it civil."

"Listen, old man," he said to Bobby Lee, "I'm not one of your boys. What was the point of keeping me on if you're throwing away the product?"

"You don't seem to get it," said Bobby Lee. "This is my company and I'll do what I want with it. PC Perfect has plateaued. You need sales, not new versions. We still might need another version. We'll talk this out next week. End of discussion. Thank ya'll for comin'."

Bobby Lee and his "boys" exchanged glances and they quickly adjourned the meeting. He exchanged stares with Don, Ed, and Mary. Karl shook his head. "I guess that's that."

When they left the conference room, Karl watched Bobby Lee get his briefcase and wave goodbye as if nothing had happened. He watched Mary walk down the stairs and listened to her shoes clapping along the floor. Then he walked down the stairs after her and sat down heavily on the chair next to her desk. Mary was slight and lean. The bones stuck out on her cheeks, and she had lank blond hair which would have looked better short.

"Thanks for the support," Karl said. "You'll be rewarded somewhere for fighting the good fight, if that was what it was. I'm still not sure what happened."

"You look tired," Mary said, looking him over critically.

"I thought I knew what I was doing when I sold the company, when I stayed on, when we worked on this version. I feel angry, stupid, and duped."

"We've got to start thinking of life after PC Perfect."

"Karl Megan, version two."

"You know we all have these perfect moments or perfect times when everything works just right. We've had that. And now it's over, but maybe there's another perfect moment for us. It just can't be here." Mary pulled out an organizer. "It's not here for me."

"I thought you had to stay on."

"I think we all stayed on for the same reasons, for the product, for you. It was too early to let go. Too many memories. We need post-partum therapy."

He couldn't help laughing, but it was a laugh with sharp edges.

"Vesuvio's after work?" Karl asked. "We can lie about old times and old versions."

"It's a date," Mary said.

Karl walked up to his office and settled in front of his PC. He tried out the new version one last time. It was simple, elegant. The bits and bytes switched on and off the way the were supposed to. There was no tip-toeing around the bounds of logic or good sense.

Karl turned and watched the progression of people through the open side of his office. His programmers wandered aimlessly from one end of the mezzanine to the other. Ed stood at the top of the stairs, pensive, remote.

Karl turned back to his PC, highlighted the new version of PC Perfect and punched the "delete" key; then he started taking the framed photos down. He was late, but it was time to start working on the new version of Karl Megan.

Is That All There Is...

Norman Fellows locked the door of Fellows Investments in the Bay View Industrial Park in San Rafael, California, and walked slowly across the half-empty lot to his car. Norman started the Volvo, slipped Bach's Goldberg Variations into the CD player, and his strong bony fingers tapped counterpoint as he turned onto Lucas Valley Road and drove through the Highway 101 underpass. But on the long, straight stretch of that road, his fingers paused as if they'd struck a dissonant note, and his hands settled on the steering wheel.

Norman twisted his long neck to the right, then the left, stretching it and feeling the cervical bones rub against each other and crack. It loosened the rest of his lanky body. He felt blood rush to his face, his high cheeks and forehead, and tingle the roots of his wavy blond hair, and then he felt the blood subside, circulate. Norman was loosening up to pose the question he'd posed for the last week: was Reno—his wild, exasperating, and costly girlfriend—getting ready to take off, fly the coop, leave for parts unknown? The question had followed him like an incubus since last week at Mac Cowen's party when Mac, his neighbor, and Reno had disappeared for an hour. Unanswerable question, impossible scenario. Was it the cliché of the eternal triangle, the rutting bucks, the prize doe? It didn't matter; what mattered was that he felt the couple known as Norman and Reno was dissolving into its elements. Element Norman would manage his clients' investments, catalogue the native plants in his small but intriguing patch of the natural world and find Reno II, or better, an anti-Reno, someone sedate and aggressive, a real estate agent named Ricki, perhaps. Element Reno would party with Mac, paint her increasingly moody pictures, then likely find someone else too. That would be Mac II or III or someone named Thor, a Hell's Angel from Oakland. The vortices of the eternal triangle spiraled inside the eternal cycle.

Lucas Valley Road had become bends and turns, brown-ish mountainside, leafed-out valley side. Norman shifted his long body first to the right then the left. The ache in his back dulled, then returned sharper. He tried to distract himself by looking for plants on the hillside. Where were the Indian paintbrush, the hidden, endangered manzanitas? Norman refocused on his hands, then the road. It was impossible not to think of what was coming up, seeing Reno, talking it out, deciding it was over. He knew—felt, lately—that it was over. It started long before Mac's party. He saw now that they had, after the newness had worn off, reverted to type. He spent more time alone, walking the woods, looking for rare plants, and planning his book. Reno painted obsessively, drank too much, and started disappearing, first for a few days, then a week.

Right turn, left turn, the steep, hard grade. The valley opened up and Norman steered away from the unprotected drop. A few minutes later, he drove towards the two houses lined up on Oak Glen's western boundary. His house was on the left, Mac Cowen's on the right. His was smaller, tidier, sedate, Mac's a rambling leviathan with a kidney-shaped pool.

Mac was a pornographer, an Internet millionaire—the

concept was so remote, so surreal. Norman shook his head, ran his hand through his hair, and felt it fall over his high forehead. He eased his Volvo next to Reno's VW. He aimed the garage door beeper over his shoulder, and the garage door rumbled shut behind him. Soon he was in a living room criss-crossed by sunlight. Through the laser teepee were the French doors, the patio, a hint of white fence, and Reno.

Reno heard him, raised herself on her elbow, and waved.

He looked at the door to his study, then decided he had to join her. He mixed a martini and threaded his way through stands of furniture and rugs to the patio. The flagstone patio tapered off into a slender quarter-acre of grass rimmed by a fence of white rough-hewn logs. Beyond the fence was a pasture with knots of Holsteins. Reno watched him come out, but then he heard a door bang next door. From where he stood, he saw Mac's patio and pool over the weathered wood fence. He didn't see Mac, but beside the pool were the usual party leftovers: empty glasses, full ashtrays, and a plate with a half-eaten hamburger.

Norman sat, tasted his martini, then said, irritably, "I keep thinking a kind man in a white coat will shake my shoulder and say that I'd been sleepwalking."

"It's funny to see you irritated," said Reno, bemused. "You two should kiss and make up." She shook a cigarette out of the pack, lit it, then settled back into the pillows of a redwood deck chair. She blew a stream of smoke towards the white sky and the green bank of oak that shored up the valley beyond the pasture.

Reno's fingers twined her already curly hair into a snarl, a gesture she made when she was worried. She wore cutoffs, a work shirt knotted around her waist, five sapphire studs in her left ear, and a dragon's-head ring with a fire opal for a tongue. They hadn't talked about the night of the party, but it was in the background waiting for them to dig it out. "It's a question of fitness and context, I suppose," he said, finessing her sarcasm.

"'Context? You mean our good neighbors?" She punched a cushion into the side of the chair and angled her round buttock into it. Then she posed her hand so the fire opal cast flickers of orange on the patio floor. "Look, Norman: fire, passion, and fantasy."

"Tending the eternal flame."

"Someone has to," Reno said, smirking.

Norman took a breath and said, "How's the painting?"

"I detect a change of subject," Reno said, smiling. "But what was the subject?" She quit playing with her ring and plunged her hand back into her curls.

"One of our phantom subjects." He consulted an imaginary organizer above Reno's head. "You were going to finish Face It and call the Cerudo Gallery about a show."

"Do you have to remember everything?"

"It's not hard when there's so little to remember."

A thunderclap of noise exploded from the patio next door; bottles clinked against bottles; there were one, two, three splashes in the pool. Voices chattered as if turned on by a switch. Metallica chords ripped through the soft light of the valley.

Reno looked next door. Norman forced himself to look at the valley. He squinted into the sun and saw a patch of brown dip in and out of the sunlight in the dense green at the head of the valley. He saw the tail of the deer bob once and disappear.

"Late start today," he said.

Reno turned back to him. "At least they start."

Norman felt stung and crossed his legs. He saw his face balloon and distort in his martini glass. At that moment, he saw Reno's affair with Mac as impossible and inevitable. He was rational, distant. He hated Mac. It was more than about Reno. It was about the loutish, stupid type. "When I don't see or hear him, I don't care. When I know he's over there yelling, snorting, and smoking..."

"...you get that crease in your forehead, your eyes scrunch up, and you hunch like Ichabod Crane."

"Always so melodramatic. And Ichabod Crane: as if you know what he looked like."

"He must have been a botanist. All botanists are skinny with piercing, dissecting eyes." Reno shook her head then said, "You're tangled up about something. C'mon, Norman."

Norman swallowed, then said, "The usual stuff. Me versus you. Whether you're going to take off again. Why you like the boor across the fence," he said—finally. It was out in the open, but they had a way of exposing things, then pretending they hadn't revealed a thing.

Reno looked at him as if he'd crossed the line. "And what do you want me to say? That I love being bored? And what do you want me to do? Settle in and watch you tag weeds?"

"So why continue?"

"Because we're using each other, that's why." Reno stubbed out her cigarette and slipped into a pair of pumps with big heels. She stood in front of him with her hands on her hips and sang Peggy Lee's overdone, wistful drinking song, one of her favorites: "If that's all there is, my friends, then let's keep dancing; let's break out the booze and have a ball."

"Is that all there is?" Norman said.

She leaned over and kissed him wetly on the forehead. "We both know it. I'm going to work on Face It," she said. "Have a double and relax. We'll talk later." Reno sashayed through the door. He saw that saucy swing of her hips which she parodied when she was drunk. Light crisscrossed her work shirt, shorts, and bare legs. She looked tiny in the living room.

He heard ice cubes rattle and vodka splash, then he heard Reno's pumps tapping up the staircase. Reno's drinking was disturbing, a symptom, worse. He was at a cusp—they were at a cusp—and Mac was a placeholder, a catalyst. Couldn't he still hate him? He couldn't imagine Mac and Reno in bed together. His Reno, their time, their memories.

Norman went to his study. He took out the cuttings he'd collected last weekend and tried, as he had for the last few nights, to identify the plant he'd discovered on the Old Growth Ridge on the weekend. The identification keys didn't help. He called Glen Kingdon, the botanist he was working with at Davis, and they decided to meet on the weekend and find and look at the plant together in rerum naturum. He was about to enter his findings into his database when he heard Reno's voice. It was thin, remote, "Let's keep dancing and break out the booze, my friend."

***

At dinner that night, Norman felt dour and, naturally, Reno matched his mood with her own bright one. She was charming, sang snatches of Ella Fitzgerald and Billy Holiday, but every time he tried to be serious, she came back to Peggy Lee and that drinking song. Racket from Mac's party—Mac's week-long party—erupted in the silences, filled the interstices, grated on his ears, made his heart pump faster, made the blood rush to his head. After dinner, he tried to go back to his study, but Reno grabbed his arm and gave him a tour of her studio, almost as if she were trying to prove she was working. Realist, expressionist, a forgettable minimalism, her latest phase was her martyred Egon Schiele one. Her latest painting, Face It, was a barely disguised self-portrait, taller and thinner than Reno, dark limbs edged with the slightest red, lips blue and curled around some inner torture.

"This can't be autobiographical," he said.

"Doesn't matter where it comes from," said Reno.

"It's too German, too melodramatic."

"Maybe you're right. Maybe I won't finish it," she said, seriously, hands on hips.

"I just meant it wasn't you."

"Part of me. Do you know me so well?"

"I guess the answer is no."

"The right answer is, let's have a ball." She did want to play, and for the first time in weeks, he found himself tangled up with her in bed. Her breasts jiggled, and her legs wrapped tight around him as if it were their first night in her shotgun shack in the tiny town of Point Reyes Station. She was warm, sloshed, and told him, laughing, that he looked more rangy and Ichabodish than ever, and whipped her curls from side to side, as if she were making fun of their love-making.

Just as he came, he realized she was asleep. His tightened, arched body, her limp form. Even when they were together, when they seemed the most like the old Norman and Reno or a perfect moment of Norman and Reno, they ended on the wrong note. He withdrew and watched her turn on her side and put her hands under her head. He covered her and dimmed the light.

The main part of the living room was dark and shadowy. Light from Mac's party flickered in the windows on the north. He poured a glass of brandy and walked upstairs to a window near Reno's studio. The party lights blazed, the heavy metal cranked up, the splashing and hooting from the pool like unsupervised grade-schoolers. The gauze of the curtains made the scene unreal. Two ghostly bikers in spangles and leather caps passed a joint, threw their heads back, laughed; a woman in a print dress plopped down on a deck chair, dropped her drink, and fell asleep, her legs drawn up in a semi-crouch. Revelers and witless energy. He disliked it by instinct; it was undirected, brutish, witless, but he could see Reno over there toasting the night, chasing invisible threads through the chaos.

Mac walked out on the patio. He was gross, a braggart. His head was large and rough, dark hair covered his face like a mask, and there was a gap between his two front teeth, like Ernest Borgnine. Mac: Internet pornographer, millionaire. In some unaccountable way, his enemy, the other buck.

When he found out who Mac was, he was stunned, curious, and amused. Internet pornographer? Oak Glen was lawyers, doctors, developers, and the stray investment counselor. He'd suspended his disbelief, and last week they went to Mac's housewarming. There were clots of Hell's Angels, punks, and guitar players; there were dealers with milky eyes and bony hands, and, of course, bags of dope, tiny pyramids of coke, and smaller doses of ecstasy and meth. Reno, of course, did everything, or tried to. She smoked, snorted, drank, danced, flirted—he expected it, especially when she got loaded—but then she disappeared with Mac. When she came back, he took her home, but then, at four in the morning, he heard Mac. Mac was swaying on his diving board, waving a half-full bottle and swearing at him for kidnapping Reno. Since then, there were hurried phone calls, Mac's partying; he was sure Reno was at Mac's in the afternoons. Another day, another suspicion. Sometimes he just wanted it to be over.

Norman rubbed his nose, closed his robe around himself, and listened to the catcalls and splashes next door for a few minutes before going to bed.

***

The road, the ride. The morning was bright and sunny, clear and cool. Norman took his time on Lucas Valley Road. He enjoyed the slow drive, the morning freshness, the bushtits and chickadees tumbling over each other in the mass of laurel leaves. If he could stay in transit, if he could somehow extend the road east past San Rafael, if that road kept unraveling...

In his office, he checked Wall Street—he had feeds from Reuters, NASDAQ, Bloomberg—read the financial reports of a score of companies, and late in the morning called his broker and bought and sold shares for several of his clients. He noted everything on the elaborate spreadsheets then wrote reports of what he'd done. He was thorough at what he did—he enjoyed being thorough. Thorough, logical—but those thoughts brought him back to the illogical, the irrational, which was the mismatch of Norman and Reno.

That afternoon, the traffic was light on Lucas Valley Road. The morning mood of escape had evaporated. He played Schumann's Carnaval. It was wistful, happy, and sad. It made him think of the best times with Reno, then the worst, then last week. There was Reno's drinking, Mac, her sad song, the unfinished painting. They were symptoms of change, a change they were both resisting. Last night they brought it out in the open then hid it under a song.

He dropped into low gear for the steep grade, when an ear-splitting horn filled the car. Klieg-like lights flashed in his mirror, and he made out a black truck with a grill that stuck out like dentures. Mac cut around him recklessly, the horn beating out a harsh staccato. An oncoming car bore down on Mac. Mac cut back in and fishtailed, sprayed gravel from the shoulder, then finally got his beast of a truck under control and raced over the crest.

And there Mac was again. The other buck. He was everywhere, waiting, ready to lock horns, his witless party perpetual, his presence a growing irritation.

At Oak Glen, Reno's VW was in the garage but she wasn't inside. He guessed where she was, and he guessed it was time. He felt lightheaded as he fixed himself a drink and went to the patio and listened to the party: that day it had started early. Was she that well-known next door that she could party without Mac being there? Had she gone over when Mac drove in? He watched the blue-white sky, a cow grazing, the hills beyond the valley, but the party made him feel he was a stranger in the middle of a carnival.

After half an hour, he heard the door, the tapping of shoes, ice cubes, pouring. Reno sat down heavily across from him. She slipped her thongs off, dug her toes into the cushion, and posed her glasses on her nose.

He nodded towards Mac's house, "How's the party?"

Reno's hand tunneled into her curls. "Fine." Reno looked nervous, then she said, "I suppose you're wondering about me and Mac. We've had a few drinks in the afternoon. We took a hike last week. He's not a bad guy. It's just that you two are polar opposites."

Norman felt his throat clench. He drained his martini and kept the glass, interested, briefly, in its broad cone. He picked out the whiff of gin which remained. His hand shook as he put the glass on the table. "He is your type."

"Mac's just a guy, a smelly average guy who has soul."

The "soul" crack pissed him off. "What is soul—pornography?"

"If you don't know, Norman, you'll never know."

"You sound like a soap opera."

"We need a little soap once in a while. We can't always be cool and rational."

"How would you know what was cool and rational? I guess it was inevitable. I saw it coming, but then I didn't know what to do about it."

"What was inevitable?"

"Your playing, your migrating to the perfect party place. I suppose you were worried about losing your studio space." He regretted he'd said it, but he knew he couldn't stop.

"It was more than that once," Reno said, seriously. "You know that."

"At least you'll be in the neighborhood and not some cantina in Tijuana."

Reno threw her glass at him, missed, and it shattered on the flagstone. Vodka spotted his shirt. Reno sprang up. "Ichabod. So it's finally cracking up."

He rubbed a wet spot of vodka. "Not cracking up. We can talk..."

"It's over, Norman. Don't you see that?" Reno turned towards the door and he reached for her, but she turned and left. He heard the door shut and her VW start up.

They both knew it, but neither could say it—until now. Was it really over? They'd said things before, then forgotten. He didn't want her to go, but then there was Mac. He went to his study and tried to enter last week's observations in his flora database, but after a few entries, he stopped. Why should he pretend everything was normal?

To go, to stay. To start writing his book. They would part; it would be sad, then life, inevitably, would march on. It was too cut-and-dried, too inhuman. Had he imagined everything? Mac and Reno: a couple of hikes, a couple of drinks—did that add up to a final split, or was that just an excuse? Ambivalence took root in his soul. After an hour, he left to find her. A couple of times when they fought, Reno had gone to Nic's Retreat, the last roadhouse in California, according to the sign.

He didn't see her VW, but he stopped anyway. "Marilyn," he said to the small woman behind the bar. "You know Reno, petite, cute, big curls, lots of jewelry?"

Marilyn was slight with black straight hair and a sad

face. "Haven't seen her." It was a dead night. The restaurant had two active tables and a bar with an old man with a shiny bald head and dressed in jeans and work boots. "It's too late to find her anyway," he said.

"You sound too sad. It's never too late," Marilyn said, trying to reassure him.

"Maybe," he said, wondering if it were true.

He watched the light stream through the open door. A milk truck from the Point Reyes dairies lumbered around the Nicasio bend, disappeared, then reappeared on the sinusoidal road. A too-serious, lanky naturalist and a firecracker of a party girl. It was doomed from that first meeting in the funereal bar in Point Reyes Station.

He came in after ten.

Reno was gone, some of her clothes gone, Face It and some of her paints gone. She'd waited until he left and come back. That had happened before too.

He stayed up late listening to the harsh music from next door. He felt like a wraith, a ghost condemned to roam a vacant space, searching for surcease. He felt oppressed by the size of the living room. He saw his image reflected in windows. He looked long and lean, haggard, worried. He could have predicted everything, but then he couldn't. Last night they'd made love; tonight it was over. He thought of Face It, the long limbs, the edging of red, the staring, tortured look. He tried to sleep but couldn't. He watched the party next door hoping he wouldn't see Reno, sure he would. He thought he did, but when he parted the curtains, it wasn't her.

The next day he drove to work woodenly, the road a drab irritation. He canceled an appointment in the city and went through his address book and phoned everyone who knew Reno. He'd done it before; no one had seen her.

He drove home, but couldn't muster the energy to play a DVD. Reno and Norman. They were on very different life tracks, sometimes crossing, mostly separated by moods and timing. He saw her soft brown eyes, her tangle of curls, her ring flashing.

Suddenly Mac pulled up behind him, horn blaring, and Norman felt anger spread through his body. He felt the blood rush to his head. Norman gripped the wheel with his left hand and with his right punched the horn. Norman saw the truck turn down the hill in the opposite lane and the turnout on the right, near the sharp bend. He saw the edge of the narrow shoulder; there was a hundred-foot drop, jumbled, pointed rocks below.

He would wave Mac on and, as Mac passed, he would speed up and keep Mac in the other lane for an extra second. Mac would be buried in the grill of the oncoming truck, or he would turn towards the hundred-foot drop. Gravel would spray up like a rooster tail and, for a moment, Mac's truck would be motionless, as if it were a huge kite flown by a distant child. Then, silently, Mac and his truck would plunge over the side. The truck would smash into the pointed rocks.

Norman felt an intense, fearful joy. A drop of sweat angled past his ear. He raised his hand to wave Mac on, his foot poised on the accelerator. But then, frantically, he dropped his hand and accelerated so Mac couldn't pass. A second later the truck whistled past like a locomotive. A few seconds later, Mac passed him, shook his fist, and was gone.

Norman skidded into the turnout at the crest and his car

was enveloped in dust. Through the dust, he watched Mac's truck turn into Oak Glen in the valley below. A wave of the hand, a slight pressure. A chill ran through Norman's body that he'd thought of causing Mac's death, that he thought it would do any good.

He looked at Oak Glen. There was his patio, a stretch of green, a bank of oak, an empty living room.

Was that all there was?

THE OPENING

I'm not sure what I am. I was a painter. Call me an art-vampire; call me Dorian's shadow.

I'm short, iron rail-thin, black-butch, thick-veined, Sicilian. I was a successful painter, had a full bank account and a small coterie of admirers, patrons, and gallery owners.

My flat and studio is on Nob Hill in San Francisco, closer to the old grandeur of Grace Cathedral and the Fairmont than the cesspool of Polk Gulch. I used to walk by the Vesuvius Gallery on Clay Street and admire my timed slashes on the gallery walls. I painted edgy Pollocks, red-rimmed Styls...stylized madness filtered through smug Midwestern eyes for pastel walls. I hinted at violence with red slashes on shiny whites and blacks, occasionally adding a homespun calculation of existential angst, the vacant eye, the faceless face. But I knew where the money was. My paintings were never too outré.

My friends—a loose group of Art Institute kids, struggling artists, and wannabes—wondered about my taste for the secret violence and estrangement in man's soul. They nodded wisely over their lattes as they compared my paintings to Bacon's huddled red implosions, Nolde's frenzy, or Schiele's naked blood-rimmed torsos.

Before the incident, I used to think I could fuse the inner and outer, the left and right brain, the object and subject with my own peculiar slant. That was the theory, the Apollonian explanation. I lived close to Grace Cathedral, but my inspiration was Polk Gulch.

Late that day, I gravitated to Polk Gulch. I sat at the window of the Gulch Saloon. Behind me pool balls clicked and drunks spouted eternal verities. Outside it was the usual lust-chasing-the-edge-of-night, worn leather, hairless chests, pink skulls, and green spike-heads. Hawks picked up chickens, and chickens faced off in dark alleys. The street moved across the canvas of my eye. It was my carnival, a mockery, their faces my masks, their violence my timed slashes.

He was short, a plump Diego Rivera; dark hair fell like a sheaf over a simple brown eye. He garbled a threat. I glanced quickly up the street. No police cruisers. I shrugged and dug out my wallet. Simple enough. It was stupid; it was over. I would regard the scene with a new strain of cynicism; he would lose himself in Polk's stained fresco.

My brown-eyed Rivera looked at me, a smile tugging at his mouth, and slashed up at my face. It must have been instinct, or he saw something, perhaps arrogance. Perhaps he saw I didn't care or would survive…I watched the fingerling blade in his brown fist hang against the dark shadows of the alley, and then he was gone, slipping into the shadows.

The blood slipped through my hand. A drop splashed on the pavement like an exploded circle.

Then there were police, ambulance, St. Francis Hospital, ER's blinding white.

In the mirror, I saw a stitched scratch across my cheek.

I'm thick-skinned, cynical. I was okay. Incident over.

I sold a painting I'd already finished of whites and blacks with my red hints; I sold another with the same edgy background but with a cluster of Ensor masks in the foreground, carved and shiny like merry-go-round horses.

I misjudged my confidence. I dreamt of fingerling knives and brown eyes. I saw the outline of a real artist through the cut. The eyes in the mirror darkened and hollowed as I touched my wound. I spread it with my fingers and saw behind the stitches a long scab, brown like the cut on a baguette. I paced through my studio and began to see my red scrapes as false, a sell-out.

I haunted Polk Gulch. At first, I thought I had to find my little Rivera, face up to him, dare him. No. His fingerling knife was real and I was not. My scar was real, my red slashes not. When I put my finger on my scar, I was touching art.

I was sitting in the Gulch Saloon when I heard the ambulance. My stomach felt empty as I hurried up the hill towards the sirens.

Cars sped on Van Ness and bounced lights off shop windows. I rushed towards the crowd but stopped at an alley in the middle of the block. Thick splashes wove out of the alley like red snakes.

I followed the snakes. Snakes with feet: right foot red, left a hollow print; right foot red, left a hollow print. Each square of gray pavement had a jagged line of red winding through it. The squares were paintings, rough, ragged, but true, real. The street was a huge gallery, the squares paintings.

Inside the crowd, I found a slight man. His bare chest was slashed, his body pale, limned with night shadows. His hollow eyes fixed mine from inside a cone of white uniforms. He was a real artist, a real Shiele, a real Bacon.

Another opening on the street.

GARAGE SALE

Bodi surprised me when he announced in a measured tone that he was moving permanently to his mother's farmhouse near Pella, Iowa. This pronouncement would have been a surprise coming from anyone who had lived in San Francisco for twenty years, but coming from Bodi it was an earthquake.

Bodi—in his twenty years in the City—had grown from a lean twenty-year-old into a dyspeptic urban Kringle, a figure whose apocryphal gruffness, petulance, and binges had alienated all but the most hardened friends, whose presence as the fiery manager of the Fell Apartments was fixed in the eye of Hayes Valley, whose absence would trigger a fleeting sense of unease.

The inevitable garage sale was held in the horseshoe courtyard of the Fell Apartments. The building itself was a testament to a ship's carpenter who had built odd-shaped apartments with close-fitted nooks and crannies as if the building were a boat and the tenants different-sized sailors. The building was close to Market Street and Van Ness, but hidden, as if that ship's carpenter had fashioned a place where he—and Bodi later—could spin out his eccentricities in peace.

They spread Bodi's stuff—mostly books—over tarps on the ground and the basement stuff from dead or gone tenants over tables and planks, making the courtyard a Germany after the Allied bombing, where everything was outdoors because there was no indoors.

The basement stuff smelled of water, dirt, and years, and people stared and picked up objects as if they'd fallen from Mars. It was mostly bric-a-brac, piles of rusty silverware, yellowed letter openers, pressed corsages under glass, coasters, broken games, plants. There were oddities: surf boards grooved by squads of mice, whiskey bottles shaped like red-cheeked English lords, a wilderness toilet, seven paintings of sunflowers by J. Montrose, a porcelain of an aging lusty centaur whose hairy legs trapped a Rubenesque woman whose nipples blinked red on and off.

The sale was one of small stories: a serious bargainer left to get money and never returned; a thin waitress at a Brazilian disco needed jade plants; a couple had to have that wilderness toilet. It was a sprawling story of nods and messages passed over the courtyard from eyes and hands; it was a story of curiosity, wonder, and indefinable pauses as people caught glimpses of their own unfinished time as they picked over the remains of Bodi's twenty years.

Bodi enjoyed reciting the history of the oddities—at first. Then he was at the edge of the sale, picking up this piece or that, knowing what it was intimately, wondering, I supposed, what that courtyard debris meant in the grand scheme. It was almost dark when we went to Bodi's room.

His room—formerly a retreat of maps, posters of California wildflowers, photo collages, books, stuffed hawks, and old clocks—had the leaving mystique. The books were in boxes, the bookshelves removed, everything else packed or shipped. Old newspapers papered the walls where the bookshelves had been. We sat on a floor of garbage-can liners, book covers, and discarded photos; a few sat on the bed, which was the bottom drawer of a chest from that ship's carpenter.

Tenants from the Fell Apartments said their goodbyes and talked of the old days. Bodi's face was philosophical, as if he were composing a suitable valedictory.

Don said, "Remember when you told your boss off?"

George said, "...and dropped that wine bottle?"

Bob said, "...and threw that coleus at Pam?"

Bodi got up, as if he were acting out a thought, pulled up the window, and yelled at one of the Fell Street irregulars who was pissing in the courtyard. It was a ritual we'd all witnessed.

Later, on the roof, the wind blew cold through our windbreakers. Bodi brought a kite we hadn't sold, and it caught in the wind. He unrolled the line slowly through his thick fingers as if he were one of the Sisters unrolling a life.

He held the empty spool for a long second before letting it go. The kite jerked in the air as if invisible demons fought over it. Then it dove towards Market Street and vanished.

We all thought it was important and nodded. Bodi said it was letting San Francisco go. It was symbolic, he said, and we should have known it before we asked.

Back in his apartment, four of us talked about when Bodi came to the city.

"Did you have a dream?" Don asked.

Bodi shook his head and looked at the boxes of books as if they contained a dream which had eluded him for years. "Everyone has a dream."

"Now?"

"Nothing's changing," said Bodi. "Nothing's changed."

"Leaving is being reborn," Bob said.

"Turner's thesis in reverse," said Don.

I left late that night. In the courtyard, a homeless man zipped up his zipper and scuttled off into the night. I turned and regarded the empty courtyard. I wondered whether, one day, Bodi would have another garage sale in Pella, Iowa.

I turned and left, thinking of Bodi, detritus, and garage sales and what it all meant. I decided as I watched the streaming traffic on Van Ness that garage sales were a cheerless way to punctuate life.

VIRTUAL REALITY

John Marquis had been in his room for hours.

It had become cold, freezing, frigid. He turned the radiator knob. It was broken, hard to turn. Finally he listened to the water. It gurgled and clanked through the pipes. It felt as if he were starting the old building, as if that knob were the ignition and the building a rusting, leaking, junked car. It gave him a fleeting feeling of power. Control. Wasn't that his problem?

The sun had set. Thick morning fog had spread through the Tenderloin like tentacles then gradually receded, as if it were a huge octopus who had touched an enemy. When he looked out the window now, it was early evening. The whores emerged and stood at the corner of Geary and Hyde, their reflections in the Vietnamese hairdressers' window making them seem four not two. Shadow worlds. He knew about shadow worlds. For too long his life was a shadow, a pale reflection, a skittering around the edges of shrinking away.

Lately, he'd thought of his youth in upstate New York, near Blue Mountain Lake. Seemed like a long ways to San Francisco and the Tenderloin. Of course, there was school, Lubbock, Tucson, Oakland. There was a whole universe in Oakland. It all seemed strange, had seemed strange for so long. The nest, Mindy, the wife, Jenny, the daughter. And then his switch. The meth, the coke, the wandering into a different life. He'd become a shadow, a reflection on the sand. Meursault.

He picked up the gun from where he'd hidden it under the stove. A small black man missing his front teeth sold it to him yesterday for five dollars. He didn't want to buy it but did so as a favor. Said he'd buy it back today. The gun was old. It looked like a prop in an old movie. He wasn't sure it worked. He looked in the barrel, then pointed it at an empty shop across the street, curious to see if it worked. He sighted down the barrel and squeezed the trigger like a kid.

He watched the glass crumple.

Whoops. He watched people disappear from the street. He knew he'd made a mistake, a big mistake. He walked backwards into the room as if he were trying to escape what he'd done.

He was sure no one saw him. He put the gun down on the bed and retreated into the small alcove with its brown fridge, microwave, and sink. He listened. Nothing. That was good.

A distant siren got louder and louder. He knew it had stopped right next to where the two whores stood, next to the hairdresser. That was bad.

Then a stream of noise, a waterfall of noise flowed into the room and surrounded him, isolated him, as if he were the only being in the world. For a brief instant, that's how he'd felt earlier. Then he didn't feel anything, as if he were in a dream or an alternate reality, watching what the real John Marquis did. He'd felt that before; perhaps we all do. Looking out through the eyes, wondering what strange things happened out there. Then it was about control.

He knew they'd roped off the intersection, moved people out of buildings. He took off his old crimson Harvard sweatshirt.

That alternate John Marquis knew he'd fucked up-royally. But he saw, from that same distance, the lines in his face, his gnarled hands, the razor-thin body. Somewhere along the line, the line that led from college, to family, to drugs, to some crazy state, he'd lost who he was. He saw that.

He thought about The Magic Mountain. In college, he'd read it in German. TB patients dying in sanitariums, eating good food, talking, smelling flowers, reading poetry, and pointing to storm clouds over the mountains. It was a sanctuary for watchers.

Another siren wailed in the dusk and died away. The noise in the room ebbed, flowed back, a backwash to what he guessed was happening outside. The simulacrum of John Marquis wondered what to do. The gun was pointing at the TV across from the bed. He thought of zapping the TV... he'd thought of that before. He'd seen it in comics. Queer. He wondered if he were on TV. If he was, it would be like that new computer thing, virtual reality. Doing and watching yourself do at the same time. Except he was already watching himself. It would be another degree of separation.

The room was a mess. He let things stay where they dropped, leaving little piles of clothes or bills or papers. John Marquis worked his way through the piles and sat on the bed next to the gun. A bed in the living room. It wasn't civilized he told Jenny. She said it wasn't either, but there wasn't a lot he could do. You couldn't move to Russian Hill on $311 SSI a month, she said.

At least she was rational.

He wondered why he never made his bed. He liked it better when it was made but could never do it. He punched a pillow up against the wall and leaned into it. He watched the rooftop across Geary thinking someone would appear. Police shows were like that. The SWAT teams with steel helmets and plastic visors. They swarmed the rooftops like bugs.

He felt like looking at the street. Where did the sirens stop? Did they evacuate the buildings? Or—nothing. The whole thing a tempest in a teapot. They would think the shot came from a car. All over. The whores back to the corner, the tiny Vietnamese ladies with their burnished hair back into their salon. The cars circling, looking for the elusive parking place.

He walked slowly to the side of the window. He picked up the drape with his forefingers and peeked out.

* * *

"How long's he been up there?"

The policeman watched the curling drapes.

He was young but hard. His belt drooped, heavy with equipment. "Don't know. I saw him come out twice."

The first time they'd seen the curtains split apart, he saw the eye. It stared as if he were making up his mind. It was a peculiar stare, intense. The policeman had seen that stare when someone went all the way. People who go all the way dressed up, made themselves neat, as if they were going to a funeral. People who went all the way took people with them. He wasn't sure why. He'd always wondered about that. It made him think that he couldn't understand some people. Some people were beyond the pale. Beyond the pale. It was a phrase his wife used when she met someone she didn't like. Going all the way. It didn't help the person going out. Did

135

they feel better for a second? Did that justify their life or what they were doing? People who decided to go all the way were beyond the pale.

The man opened the curtains again, wider. He looked puzzled and laughed. The policemen tensed, then relaxed when the curtains curled over the emptiness.

"How long has he been up there?"

The policemen looked at a small man with the baggy eyes. "Too long."

The streets in back of the lines were full of people. They drifted in wearing housecoats and sneakers, then drifted away as if they'd left something better on TV.

"Who is it?" said a woman in curlers. The policeman watched the window. The negotiator arrived and yelled into his bullhorn, asking John Marquis to come down.

John Marquis came to the window. He was dressed up and had that queer look.

"How long has he been up there?"

* * *

John Marquis knew he'd have to explain what happened. He had this gun. He didn't know it was loaded. Blah, blah, blah. There'd be police, handcuffs. It had happened before.

First he had to eat, then he had to dress. He went to the kitchen.

Piles everywhere. He put down a paper towel. He took white bread out of a tiny fridge and put two slices next to each other on the paper towel. He brought out a half a round of cheddar cheese and cut off two thick wedges and laid them side by side on one slice. He carefully put everything back in the fridge and put the empty slice of bread on the one with the cheese.

It stuck to the roof of his mouth—why did he always think it wouldn't? He poured himself a glass of milk. He drank half of it and moved his tongue around the edges of the bread until it loosened and fell into his mouth. He took the glass into the living room to check the roof.

The roof was empty. But the intersection was roped off with that thin black-and-yellow tape. In back of the tape were policemen, police cars, and people.

He brushed his teeth, then shaved, lathering his face, then carefully shaving the lather off. He watched it swirl down the drain with pieces of bread and cheese.

He dressed with his best clothes, his one clean shirt.

Magic Mountain. If only he could. But now we had a substitute. He wrote the words "virtual reality" on his mirror with a pencil. It hardly showed.

Someone called his name. It sounded loud and hollow. He walked slowly back through the piles. He picked up the TV remote. If only life were like the TV. You could stop and start it. You could in virtual reality. Start and stop. If only you could do that with life.

He walked to the window. Zap, zap, zap.

Behind him the TV popped on. John Marquis turned and saw the man on the roof on TV.

"It's on! Hah. Maybe I'll be on!"

John Marquis happily aimed the remote at the window but glanced at the TV.

"What's taking them so long?"

Zap, zap, zap.

"There I am! There I am! I'm so washed out. I've got to get close to the window."

Zap, zap, zap.

The room exploded.

John Marquis was on.

HOME

I finished conducting a late tour of the arboretum and, as the garden closed up, decided to linger. I've been doing that more lately since Dad died. No, that's not right. I try to be clear about this when I think about it, but I'm never sure when I'm lying to myself. Not lying but glossing over the truth. The truth is I've been staying outside more—lingering— since the estate was settled, the house sold, the effects gone. It's about the house.

Lately I've had this feeling of loss, deep loss, when I leave the garden and am swallowed in the traffic, buses, and hurry of San Francisco. When I flip the lock on my apartment, it seems the outside world, the world of plants and trees and open skies, disappears, becomes a kind of illusion.

I watched the guard drive slowly through the gardens telling people it was closing, and they started drifting towards the east or north gate. It was spring and the sun was bright in the west and starting to etch shadows on the east side of the big Monterey cypress, which anchored the big lawn. The French romantic vistas began to empty of people and became quiet hourglasses.

The park people know me and let me stay, knowing I can always leave through the after-hours turnstiles. I started walking away from the east gate. I walked past the cypress and across the great lawn but stopped in the middle. I saw a woman hurrying towards a thick tangle of sinuous leptospermum, which hugged the arboretum on the north.

She stopped, turned, and watched me. She was thin-nosed, big-eyed, and slender. I'd talked to her before about feeding the feral cats. She'd wait until the garden closed, then, because of her size, she'd slip through the bars of the east gate carrying her bags of cat food. I'd seen where she'd set up a feeding station deep in the leptospermum, where she'd scattered tins of food and water so the cats wouldn't fight. We stared at each other. Her eyes challenged mine. That day, feeling a curious sense of my own abandonment, I turned away.

The arboretum used to be home to an abundance of songbirds, woodpeckers, and had five quail coveys, now one, soon none. But I understood her that day. She was making a home for the cats, feeding them, helping them survive. She thinks it's a noble thing. That day I couldn't fault her.

I walked down the gentle slope towards the turtle pond and paused briefly to watch the gulls and coots and mallards making circles in the water. Then I turned and took the dark path between the New Zealand and Australia section and passed between the New Zealand Christmas Tree with its thick aerial roots hanging down like old brooms and the Australian Doranthes with its high red toothbrush. When I lead tours I say, "Now we're walking between Australia and New Zealand," and everyone laughs.

I walked slowly into Chile and strolled by fields of alstromeria, the Lily of the Incas, in rainbow bloom, softer in the fading light. I stopped in Central America at the insidious monkey hand tree with its red and yellow flowers twisted into what would be a weapon in a Holmes murder.

In the succulent garden, the puya was coming into bloom. It was an outer-space plant with its blue fleshy leaves and orange flowers. The cacti and aloes, even though the light was fading into shadows, were still being dive-bombed by hummingbirds who mapped their territories in swinging arcs.

I sat on a bench off the nature trail. Distant gulls spiraled towards Ocean Beach; a Red-shouldered Hawk settled into a nest high in a Monterey pine. The sun, despite the longer days of spring, was sinking fast, brushing the trees with gold, and making longer shadows.

Finally, with a feeling of regret, I left. I walked slowly towards the after-hours gate, not wanting to leave the colors, scents, and twisting spaces of my garden.

At the after-hours gate, I found a couple in Day-Glo spandex looking sorrowfully at a tandem bike. The bike was too long to get through the revolving gate.

One reason, I said, bikes aren't allowed.

They were apologetic—which was rare—and I helped them. We went to the place where the stone wall is low and the drop easy. They jumped down, and I lowered the bike to them.

I went to the after-hours gate and walked slowly past where they'd jumped down, then past the main garden entrance, up to the stoplight.

I always look back.

I never like to leave, but I especially didn't want to leave that day. I could already feel the tug of the crowds on Lincoln, and beyond was the streetcar with its heavy metal-on-metal screams. If you take the historical tack, the park is artificial. A century ago, it was sand dunes. Now it was transplanted Australian, New Zealand, Chilean...whatever. I usually don't think of the sand dunes. There has to be a historical statute of limitations.

It's hard to be objective: I was leaving my ground, the place that was home. No one knows anymore where they feel at home. We do things and pretend we live in places that aren't quite human, which don't quite fit.

A car stopped near the crosswalk. A tall dark-haired man with thin legs got out. He opened the back of a fastback.

He took out a boom box and placed it carefully next to the garbage can. Then he unloaded packages wrapped in plastic grocery bags and stuffed them inside the can until white bags stuck out the sides like a mushroom with a black helmet. He piled on more clothes and bags and a small sway-backed futon.

He finally saw I was watching him. He looked at me for a moment and said, "I got that job. I've been waiting for a real apartment for a long time."

www.ingramcontent.com/pod-product-compliance
Lightning Source LLC
Chambersburg PA
CBHW070336130626
46556CB00007B/2888